SCIENCE FICTION GEMS

Volume 1

ISAAC ASIMOV
and others

I0616863

ARMCHAIR FICTION
PO Box 4369, Medford, Oregon 97504

For more information about Armchair Books and products, visit our website at…

www.armchairfiction.com

Or email us at…

armchairfiction@yahoo.com

EXPLORE MAN'S FUTURE POTENTIAL

"Coffin Ship" and "Quarantined Species" will introduce you to the trepidations of deep space travel.

"The Show Must Go On" chronicles the sad tale of Man's decline in the name of profit and entertainment, while "Living Space" offers a look into the consequence of arrogance.

"Chicken" and "Subject to Change" will challenge your objectivity and make you question the very safety of your surroundings…

All these and more will take you on a trip with exciting authors of yesteryear, and today. Discover fascinating options, horrifying realities and sometimes…man's unconscionable actions.

TABLE OF CONTENTS

The Coffin Ship

By
BILL WESLEY

Cy Munson was a lone man awake on a star-ship where everyone else sleep. Why had he awakened? And if someone had had to awaken, why did it have to be the one person who knew nothing about the ship, and had no idea of what he was supposed to do?

CY MUNSON'S first awareness was of a faint whirring sound coming through miles and miles of cotton. He struggled to dissolve the cotton, then there was nothing but space— limitless black space, and the whirring sound coming from somewhere beyond. He sent out long tentacles, searching, listening, feeling. Nothing but space. He pulled them in, sent them out in other directions. Nothing but space. Space and the whirring sound. Nothing else? Yes. There was something. A faint light, like a distant star. He sent a tentacle toward the star. It was spinning, blinking—like a sun with one black side, rotating. It grew larger. He drew in his tentacles. He could see it clearly now. It wasn't a sun. It was a light. A yellow, blinking light; and it was right over his chest.

He closed his eyes tightly, then opened them again, concentrating on the light. It stopped blinking and he saw that it was a push button. Under it was a printed sign. Munson strained his eyes, his brain, and slowly read the words, *Push this button immediately on awakening.*

He tried to flex his fingers. They seemed lifeless, as did his arms. He twisted his body to see he was free. He felt nothing—no bonds, no clamps… He forced his fingers to move — only a little at first, then more as his blood circulation picked up. Slowly he bent his arm at the elbow and placed his index finger on the yellow button. Then, summoning all his strength, he pushed.

A softer, brighter light came on all around him and the yellow light went off. He saw other push buttons, and other printed signs; and he saw the walls of the "coffin".

HE MOVED his head from side to side, checking his physical coordination and looking for the source of the whirring sound. A faint breeze stirred against his cheek; it came from a vented opening beside him. The whirring was the sound of an air conditioner. Slowly, and with great effort, Cy Munson read the other printed signs.

Lie still until you feel strength in your muscles. Talk to yourself if you like. Try not to sneeze or cough.

Regulate temperature with this dial.

Do not become impatient. Automatic controls have already been triggered. If you are the first to awaken there will be a delay of fifteen minutes while the outside chamber is brought up to living conditions. You will be released automatically when it is safe.

This is a third level compartment. When released, you will find yourself four feet above the floor. Watch your step.

Emergency button. Depress only if you feel extreme discomfort, or if thirty minutes has elapsed since pressing yellow button.

Thirty minutes? How would he know? He had no watch. Was he supposed to count? He could hardly think; where the devil was he anyway?

Vaguely Munson remembered climbing aboard the spaceship. He remembered the crowd, waving—the television cameras—"Old Beanpole" Simpson smiling at him from the speakers' platform...

GRADUALLY, memory came to him, then realization. He was in a spaceship bound for—bound for where? What the dickens was the name of the place? Capella. That was it. Supposed to be like the sun —and with planets, the scientists said, at least three, maybe more. And it was going to take sixty

6

years to get there; that explained the suspended animation. But why Cy Munson? He was no scientist; he had even had a rough time with Physics 1A while squeezing through NU on his football scholarship. How the devil had he gotten mixed up in such a deal?

Then he remembered Simpson again, the managing editor of the Chicago *Planet*—remembered the day he had gone ranting through the city room shouting, "A million bucks down the drain. A million bucks we bid for an exclusive, and not a single reporter passes the physical. What a bunch of soft-bellied, whiskey-guzzling, night-owling..." He had stopped when his gaze had lit on Cy. "You there," he had shouted, letting his eyes wander over Cy's thick muscles and clean, tight skin. "What do you do? What's your name?"

Cy told him. "Munson, sir. I work in circulation."

"Ever do any reporting? Don't answer. Neither has anyone else for the past fifty years. Get over to the Space Force Development Center and tell 'em you're from the Chicago *Planet*. And pass that physical or you'll never work another day on this paper, or any other paper."

WELL, THAT was how he happened to be on the ship; he remembered that much. And he remembered the shot in the arm before being laid to rest in the "coffin" but what had happened to the sixty years? It couldn't have... Why, it had only been a minute! Like a Sunday afternoon nap, after reading the comics. If that was all there was to it...

He glanced around the tight little compartment curiously, looking for some indication of time. He didn't know what. A calendar wouldn't do any good, unless it was some kind of automatic thing...

His eye caught a moving dial. A clock—with a minute hand and a second hand. Four and a half minutes, it read the elapsed time since he had pushed the yellow button, he guessed. If so, he was in for a long fifteen minutes...

Sixty years, just like that! Munson tried to snap his fingers.

Didn't do too well. Monk, and Johnny, and "Greased" Granson, all the rest of them—eighty, eighty-five years old already, back there on Earth. Some of them dead probably. His mother and father for sure. How about Laurie? No, that was impossible. Funny little Laurie, with the cute nose, and that pert little body—she couldn't be eighty years old. She'd never be eighty years old. What a stupid nightmare...

He tried not to think of his parents, though both of them had urged him to go. "It's as much your job as anyone's," his father had told him. "It isn't easy to understand why these things are important, but Man has to keep going, keep doing, keep learning. The last man in the universe will die wondering what to do next I guess."

His mother had simply said, "Good luck, son. Try to remember at least some of the things we taught you."

And Laurie? How had Laurie taken it? She hadn't believed a word of it. "Well, go on," she had said gaily, wrinkling her nose at him. "But when you get tired dating those two-headed, furry-skinned Capellans, or whatever they are, don't come dialing my phone number again. I'm not playing second fiddle to some alien Ubangi."

SIX AND a half minutes!

"Oh, that crazy clock can't be right."

Cy Munson's voice sounded strange—thin, as if it weren't all there. He tried again. "Damn Old Beanpole," he shouted.

That was better. Had a ring to it. Made him feel good too.

"Say, maybe I will be the first guy awake. Should have had a pool on it. Ten bucks each. Eighteen guys—that'd be... Make it a hundred each. Eighteen hundred bucks. Wow! Have a deal at Vegas on that..."

What would it really be like, he wondered? Would they actually find a planet to land on? Something like Earth? With land and water—and animals—and people? Oh, that was ridiculous! He didn't know why it was ridiculous; it just was. Capella was a star. Even if it had planets, they'd be way up in the sky. How the devil could there be people and animals and trees and things way up in the sky? It just didn't make sense. Probably find... What the dickens would they find?

He hadn't the faintest idea.

One look at the Astronomy 1 textbook and he had beaten a line for Jazz Appreciation. Three units was three units. Anyway the astronomy class had met too early in the morning, and they had scheduled some overnight field trips—one of them for the weekend of the Notre Dame game. Wow! Wouldn't that have been something? How come you didn't play in the Notre Dame game, Munson? I was out looking at stars...

NINE minutes! He twisted his head around to see if there were any signs he had missed. "Ought to have a Coke machine in here," he mused aloud. Then he said, "Hey, I'm hungry. Feel like I haven't eaten for a week."

He wondered what Earth would be like when they returned. One hundred and twenty years—and six months. Six months in the Capella System—one hundred and twenty years commuting. That ought to be a record...Wow! What if we do find people there? Humans. Guys like me—and a gal like Laurie. Munson squirmed. No, he'd never find another one like Laurie. Not on a stupid yellow star. He didn't have to be an astronomer to know that much.

Eleven minutes!

He *was* going to be first, unless somebody made it in the next two or three minutes. Ought to be a special prize for the first guy awake. Extra glass of champagne, at least. That was the last thing he remembered before being shoved into the "coffin". "Champagne and caviar on Capella III when we wake up," Captain Halloran had said. "Goat's milk, you mean," someone else had said. Everyone except Cy had laughed at that. If it was a joke he had missed it. Those scientists and space force boys had their own brand of humor...

THIRTEEN minutes! He hoped his typewriter was okay. It

had better be. Old Beanpole would give him... He caught his breath. Old Beanpole Simpson was dead. Long dead. Thirty or forty years dead.

Cy felt a lump in his throat without understanding why. He hadn't even liked the guy. Domineering old bustard. "Go?" he had shouted. "Of course you'll go. The reputation of this paper depends on your going. You represent a million-dollar investment. Do you know how many words Shakespeare would have had to write to make a million dollars? Don't answer. I know: 'Who's Shakespeare?' Just write what you see—and what you feel. Don't lie. Don't exaggerate. Don't let any man in the world—not any creature in the universe—tell you what to write."

That was Old Beanpole, and Simpson had known that he would never read a word of it. Never know if it was written—or how it was written—or if there would be anything to write.

"I take it back. Old Beanpole," he said aloud. "You were quite a guy."

He counted the last minute aloud, holding his breath at the end, listening, waiting. Nothing happened.

He squirmed, looked around at the signs again. *Emergency button. Depress only if you feel extreme discomfort, or if thirty minutes has elapsed...*

Thirty minutes? Another fifteen minutes? Just lying there? Wondering? Thinking? Remembering? He'd never make it. What the devil was the matter with those scientists? They were supposed to be smart...

He began to feel uneasy. What if something had happened to the ship? Hit by a meteor maybe. One of the astronomers had mentioned that. What if he was alone in space? Torn loose from the ship by an explosion of some sort. Just him and his coffin—waiting sixty years for nothing. Oh, that was impossible! The mechanism would have been wrecked; he wouldn't have awakened at all. Still, something might have...

He heard a click. Then another click. Then a new whirring sound—stronger than the fan. A motor, pulling. A new breeze swept across Munson's forehead. The signs over his chest began moving toward his feet. No, he was doing the moving. The coffin was sliding out. It had worked. After sixty years, it had worked. He was awake and he was free.

Free somewhere way up in the sky on a stupid yellow star...

HIS FIRST thought after jumping down from the "coffin" was that something had gone wrong after all. The room was completely unfamiliar. It was larger than he remembered, and it was totally enclosed. He remembered windows—large, clear windows, through which he had watched the crowds, and had seen Old Beanpole, and the buildings of the spaceport in the distance, and beyond them the whitecaps breaking along the Florida coast. Now there were only the solid walls of the spaceship.

Maybe it was the pilot room he was thinking of...

He ran to see, bounding high in the air because of the low gravity. He had forgotten about that. Someone had tried to explain it to him before blast-off. The ship would be made to rotate, to effect an artificial gravity, but it would only be about one-fourth normal Earth gravity. Now Munson felt foolish, flailing his arms and legs in the air, waiting impatiently to come down before taking the next step.

No, the pilot room was bare too, except for the master panel set against one wall. For an instant he almost went into a panic. He was positive that there had been windows, and more than one panel, and furniture...

He spun around desperately. A new thought had worked its way into his brain and he felt goosepimples gathering on his skin. Where were the other crewmembers? Surely some of them should have awakened by this time...

HE WENT hopping back into the morgue, as the space force boys had labeled it with such malicious pleasure, cursing the delay caused by his grotesque steps, having forgotten again about the low force of gravity.

The coffins were just as he had left them—closed up tight, all except his own.

He searched the room for directions—more printed signs, or an instruction manual. Something, for God's sake…

The front of each coffin carried two meters and a dial. The meters were marked *Pulse Rate and Body Temperature*. The dials were simply marked *Index*. All the meters read zero. The dial settings ranged from three to seventeen, on a scale of twenty-five. Munson had no idea what "index" they referred to, but he knew what zero pulse rate and zero body temperature meant. They meant that no one else on the ship was showing the slightest tendency to awaken…

He groped his way back to the pilot room and started reading the markings under the meters and switches on the master panel.

Polar Coordinates, Earth's Perihelion.

It didn't mean a thing to him.

Earth Distance, L. Y.

What was L. Y.? Whatever it was, there were five of them back to Earth.

Course Velocity.

The dial went to a hundred; the needle pointed to ninety-five. He didn't learn anything from that.

Polar Velocity.

Same sort of dial. It read seventy-eight.

Viewscreens.

AT LAST. There was one Cy Munson could understand. There were three switches. *Course. Destination. Earth.*

He flipped the switch marked *Earth*, then held his breath.

A large square of light appeared on one wall and shadows began dancing over the area. After a moment, the shadows stabilized and he saw a patch of starry sky; nothing more. No Earth. No Sun—unless one of the bright stars was the sun; he had no way of knowing. Apparently they were too far away to see Earth. Well, of course! He should have guessed that. They couldn't see any of Capella's planets from Earth, could they?

Eagerly he flipped the switch marked "Destination." Another patch of light appeared. Again he held his breath while the picture formed. He had learned one thing, and he felt better for it. The windows he had remembered had been the television screens...

The streaks and shadows on the second screen stabilized and again he saw only a starry field. He glanced back and forth from one screen to the other. The stars were in different places. More bright ones on the second screen, Munson thought; otherwise they were identical, for all that he could see. Then where was the one they were shooting at? Capella? Why wasn't it blazing big and bright? And where were its three planets?

SLOWLY the realization of what had happened worked its way into his brain and he felt a shudder run up his spine. Something had caused him to awaken prematurely; he was alone in space—trillions of miles from nowhere. He didn't know how to awaken the others, and he didn't know how to get back to sleep himself. Munson was trapped—trapped and lost and scared.

Cy didn't know how long he roamed about the ship looking for some clue, some instructions, some hope. He only knew that it had seemed like days and that he found nothing—nothing, that is, that would help him out of his predicament. He found a great many things, and he learned quite a lot about the ship, but he was just as much lost as before. More so, perhaps, because now he was sure of it.

Munson found the other panels that he remembered. He brought them out of hiding by flipping switches on the master panel, the same way he had found the television screens. But the auxiliary panels only referred to external controls—radar, radio, and flight control of the ship in atmosphere. They didn't show him what he really needed.

He found relays on the master panel that would cut off the ship's oxygen pump, and other relays that would cut off the power generators. These, he assumed, had been closed automatically when he had awakened.

He found a bank of eighteen switches marked *"Subliminal Excitation"*, but he didn't know what it meant and he didn't feel that he had the right to experiment. What if he caused the ship to deviate from its prescribed course? In sixty years, or however much time was left, the ship might become hopelessly lost in space.

HE FOUND food. Crates and crates of rations—all clearly marked as to which meal was inside and how many servings. There appeared to be a hundred percent surplus over what the crew would expect to use in the six months on Capella III, or wherever they landed. That meant that he had a nine-year supply without touching the basic ration.

He had no way of judging the water supply; the tanks were concealed in some other part of the ship. He could only guess that the water supply would match the food supply; anything else would be unrealistic.

He had no way of guessing at the oxygen supply either, or at the heating and lighting potential. It worried him that each hour he spent in deliberation of what to do he might be cutting off valuable "living time" for the other seventeen men aboard.

Cy Munson felt that he had gone over the ship meticulously at least a hundred times, but his common sense told him that it had probably been closer to a dozen. He found no instructions for waking a man in suspended animation. He found no switches or dials or relays marked in any way to give him a clue. He hadn't even found a dictionary to help him decipher the markings that he didn't understand.

HE FOUND two things that were *not* helpful. One was a sign over the bank of coffins in the "morgue" which read, *It is a capital offense for anyone to touch these index dials without explicit authorization from the ship's commander.*

The other thing he found was a growing feeling inside him

that he had no moral right to try to awaken anyone else. Suppose he was able to stir up some sort of response inside one of the coffins—he still might not be able to get it open. Or what if he got it open and the man died instead of awakening? Or what if he awoke and knew no more about what to do than Cy did? Then there would be two of them and Cy Munson would be the same as a murderer...

On the other hand, he might be committing murder anyway, he told himself, if he was using up too much oxygen. He had to do something, and he had to do it quick. It was last down, two seconds to play, and the ball was somewhere out in the middle of the field...

HE MADE one last tour of the ship—the most exhaustive search he had ever made in his life. He remembered the time he had lost a new handball that someone had given him on his tenth birthday. After looking for it hurriedly all over his grandmother's garden, and trampling her flowers and weeds indiscriminately, he had then started over again, painstakingly parting each pair of stems, lifting each leaf, straightening each blade of grass. Still he had not found the handball. He remembered that his feeling of loss had not been as great as his feeling of wonder that the handball could have escaped him. That was the way he felt now. There *had* to be a solution. There absolutely had to be. Even the handball, he remembered, had turned up weeks later stuck in a gopher hole. *Somewhere on this ship there's a gopher hole,* he told himself over and over again. But...he still didn't find it.

He found the medical supplies, and the hypodermic needles with which to administer the drugs, or whatever it was that they had shot into his arm. He supposed that the drug itself was somewhere there in one of the bottles, or in several of them, waiting to be mixed. It might as well have been buried in a salt mine in Siberia, for the good it would do him.

He found a safe with a combination dial that he spent hours trying to solve, but with no success.

He found a lot of the ship's activities, but there had been no entries since a few hours after blast-off. That took away his last hope. He had wondered if various crewmembers, or the captain maybe, were aroused periodically to examine the ship during flight. Apparently not.

Munson sat down on one of the contour chairs that he had discovered folded into a compartment and fought desperately with his emotions. He was past fear now, but he was completely disgusted with himself for not having taken more interest in the ship, for not having asked more questions, for not having been bright enough to understand what they had told him.

AT LAST the solution came to him. He fought it back as long as possible; it wasn't his fault, Munson kept telling himself. Those damn scientists! They were supposed to be smart...

Finally he couldn't postpone it any longer; he knew what he had to do. He couldn't use up any more of the ship's oxygen, nor any more of its electrical power. And he couldn't die in the ship—that would be a horrible awakening for the others, his decomposed body... He went to the cabinet where he had found the spacesuits and chose one marked *Large*. He began studying it. After a while he was ready to try it on. He experimented with the oxygen supply, made sure he could control it. He examined the ship's air lock for the twentieth time, satisfied himself that he knew how to operate it. Then he went around the ship returning everything to normal. He opened the oxygen relay, cut off the power generator, deactivated the television screens, replaced the auxiliary panels and what few pieces of furniture he had used—at last he was ready. He took one last look around, then started for the air lock...

Only then did he begin to imagine the horror that awaited him. What would it be like? What would he feel, drifting out away from the ship? Would he go mad? Would he live long enough to die of hunger, or thirst; or would he suffocate as his oxygen supply diminished?

Without admitting to himself just what his intentions were, he went back to the medical cabinet and took out a bottle of chloroform. He had already noticed the spare connection on his space helmet, and had remembered what the fitting on the chloroform bottle looked like. He had guessed right—it fit.

"Probably so anybody hurt out in space can be put to sleep on the way to the aid station," he mused aloud. Then to himself Cy Munson added, *well, this is going to be a long sleep...*

CAPTAIN Jim Halloran gradually became aware of the yellow light blinking over his chest. Then he saw the red *Emergency* light blinking too. He struggled with his drug-induced lethargy and finally overcame it to the point where he was able to raise his forearm and press the button.

During the thirty seconds while the outside chamber was being blasted with the full force of the heat engines and the oxygen pumps, he tried to shake the cobwebs from his brain.

An emergency could mean any of a number of things. Some vital part of the ship could have been damaged; a short-circuit could have caused a rocket to fire, resulting in an alteration of course. A *Stop Order* or *Change Order* could have been received by the automatic radio receiver. Even an invasion by an alien force was not impossible. Any creature coming in through the air lock would set off the ship's alarm.

When his coffin slid out, Halloran was ready. He rolled to the floor, one hand hovering over his flame pistol, his eyes searching the morgue for some hint of trouble.

He saw nothing unusual, he heard nothing unusual—and that wasn't right. He should at least have heard the whining of the heat engines as they worked at twenty-percent overload to warm up the ship. And he should have sensed the low atmospheric pressure as the oxygen unit strained to bring the chamber up to normal in one minute instead of the usual fifteen.

CAUTIOUSLY, but quickly, he made his way toward the pilot room. Either someone—or some*thing*—had awakened and started up the engines; or some accident had caused them to start up by themselves. Very likely it was the latter, he thought, because just bringing the ship's interior up to normal Earth conditions would not, of itself, constitute an emergency.

He found nothing wrong in the pilot room. The heat engine and oxygen pump were making some extra noise, as if they were slightly overloaded, but not much.

Halloran felt a chill run up his spine. Someone had been in the ship within the past few minutes. Someone had warmed it up, opened the oxygen valve, then turned everything off again. That was the only explanation, and whoever it had been, he was gone—otherwise he wouldn't have turned everything off. And it couldn't have been an alien, or the emergency relay would have been tripped when he had first come in through the air lock. *Someone on the ship had just left through the air lock!*

He glided back to the morgue, glanced quickly at the meters until he came to Cy Munson's coffin. The needles of both meters were just settling back to zero.

Halloran grabbed the coffin's handles and pulled. The coffin was not sealed—it slid out into the room, empty.

DURING the ten seconds it took him to glide once again to the pilot room, Captain Halloran guessed what had happened. "The poor boob," he muttered half to himself. "Never should have let him come. Damn politics..."

He dived for the bank of switches marked *Subliminal Excitation* and flipped the second one from the left. "Better have the Doc, too," he muttered, flipping another one further over. Then he brought down one of the viewing screens and began scanning the area around the ship in a matter of seconds he had spotted the spacesuit floating a few hundred yards out.

He was just fastening down his space helmet when his first officer, Lieutenant Ralph DePauw staggered in from the morgue.

"What the hell's going on?" DePauw asked sleepily

Halloran waved in the direction of the television screen.

"Tell you later," he said clamping down on the helmet. In another moment he was passing through the air lock.

He gave himself a tremendous push with his legs as he shot out into space, then looked ahead to see if it would be sufficient. Munson was still moving away from the ship, as he would indefinitely if undisturbed. Of course he would continue along with the ship too, his momentum in one direction being independent of that in any other direction. Halloran had only to exceed Munson's own push and he would catch up with him in a matter of seconds—he only hoped that it would not be too late.

When he was close enough to grab Munson's spacesuit, Halloran jerked him around so of he could peer in through his faceplate. Then he saw the spare hose attached to the chloroform bottle. He closed the first valve, then opened the regular oxygen valve to its fullest. He began thumping Munson's arms and chest through the heavy spacesuit until, he saw signs of awakening, then he opened his repulsion nozzle and dragged Munson back to the, ship.

DePAUW and the ship's doctor were waiting for them. Halloran turned Munson over to the doctor then went aside with DePauw.

"I want printed instructions pasted on the wall here and in the 'morgue'," he said, "so nothing like this will happen again."

DePauw shrugged. "What language you want 'em printed in?" he asked sarcastically. "Baby talk?"

"That's enough of that," Halloran snapped at him, bouncing out of his spacesuit. "He may not have known what to do, but it's a good thing for us he knew what *not* to do. There are at least a dozen ways that he could have killed us, and he didn't take a single chance. That's guts, in my book, Mister. That kid can fly with me any time, anywhere; if he ever wants to try it again."

AN HOUR or so later Cy Munson was back inside his

coffin. He felt perfectly at ease this time. The doctor had explained that it had been a million-to-one-shot that had awakened him—the combination of hard muscles that had resisted the original injection, resulting in an incomplete suspension of his life processes, plus a bad connection in the subliminal excitation circuit for his coffin.

"Actually you've aged about a week in the eight years we've been out," the doctor told him. "Maybe that doesn't seem like much, but if it hadn't been for the bad connection, you would have gone on aging until you starved to death, or died of thirst. On the other hand, if you hadn't been so close to consciousness, the conditions set up by the bad connection might not have been strong enough to arouse you, and all our oxygen and electrical power might have been dissipated through your coffin. Believe me, son, unwittingly or not, you saved this expedition."

The captain, too, had patted him on the back. Even Lieutenant DePauw had patiently and politely explained the workings of the controls to him. Even if he did wake up again now, he would know what to do. But what pleased him most was the news that they were only eight years out from Earth, instead of the full sixty.

"I knew it," he said happily, as he closed his eyes and waited for sleep to come again. "I knew that little Laurie wasn't any eighty years old."

THE END

The Android Kill

By
JOHN JAKES

The android slaves, insipid pieces of metal, plastic and skin, were constructed to work and work and help men like Caffrey relax. But someone, somewhere, made this batch too perfect. Caffrey, big tough Caffrey laughed out loud at the tremendous irony of the joke as he pondered sending his ravaged ship into the burning maw of the sun.

CAFFREY slammed the great steel doors and walked forward through the gym. His bare feet slapped on the mats and the cane of iron-hard Venus jungle wood swung lightly in one hand. He wore only dirty white trousers. Sweat stood shiny on him under the glow of the ceiling lights. He cursed the ship silently for being old and run down and without any cooling units.

His beefy face moved from side to side, watching. The black eyes took in every bit of movement. He saw all that went on. It was his ticket out of the stinking world of frozen-starred space, of Class nine freighters and unholy cargos.

The slender blue-gray androids were exercising. They vaulted on the parallel bars, dangled from the rings, worked with the pulleys. Even the women and the children exercised. They did not sweat, because their bodies were not made for perspiration, but Caffrey could see their muscles twisting and shivering under the slate hides, developing.

A strange kind of noise filled the vast gym. Muted gruntings, whispers of breath, solid slaps of hands and bodies on bars and mats. The androids did not look at Caffrey. They were accustomed to slavery. They knew they had been dead when they were born.

Caffrey stopped walking. Near the left wall, two android

21

males were conversing. They leaned indolently, tiredly, against the brown wooden bars. Caffrey's face lost its flabbiness, becoming stripped of everything but purpose.

He walked toward them, conscious of his own strength. The exercising of the others went on around him. Slap and soft wind of breath and creak of apparatus. The heat was a nearly tangible cloud.

"Why aren't you two working out like the rest?" Caffrey asked slowly.

One of the androids said in a weary voice, "I'm tired. I can't when I'm tired."

Caffrey's fingers tightened on the stick. They had to be in perfect shape! *Had to be!* This was his last shipload, and by God...

He swung the stick up over his shoulder and brought it down in a blurring arc. There was a flat smacking sound. The android choked. Caffrey struck the other one, and the anger came up from his stomach like fire boiling over. He screamed at them and beat them. Again the stick fell, again, again, again...

Finally he stood back feeling the sweat running down him. He tilted his head and gulped air. "Now," he said very quietly, "now, you inhuman sonsofslate, start working..."

The two of them watched from the gray mats where they were crouched. Brief resentment was in their eyes.

Caffrey bunched his muscles and kicked. The android's head snapped backward against the bars. He grunted. Then both of them got up and walked over to the pulleys. They began to exercise, rapidly.

Caffrey laughed and walked on through the gym, not watching them any more. He went through the next bulkhead and spun the lock wheel, then padded down the corridor under the ceiling lights that shone like foggy blue eyes.

Dillman, his astrogator, a young kid with yellow hair and an aggressive jaw, was in the chart room. He was working with the course computer. Dillman had been a student at the University of Venus, Cloud City, when he killed an officer of the Control

Police in a fight over a girl. Dillman was good in the slave game. Dillman was getting hard.

Caffrey closed the door. It clanged loudly. Dillman looked around.

"Hello, Captain," he said. "We're right on course. Mars in six hours, fourteen minutes."

Caffrey nodded, slumping down into a thickly padded shock chair. Beyond the wide observation window, space made endless black, and stars hung there like pieces of a broken diamond. The swollen ball of the sun burned above the ship, and Mars lay scarlet, just ahead. Distant rumbling from the old corroded jet tubes filled the room.

"How's everything?" Caffrey asked. "Engines?"

"All right," Dillman said, leaning against the astrogation table. "Few pieces of stuff failed to fission awhile back, but everything's okay now."

Caffrey waved his hand. "Get out the bottle."

DILLMAN grinned and pulled open a green metal wall cabinet. He filled two tumblers with the syrupy swamp wine and handed one of the glasses to Caffrey. The captain of the ship drank half, breathed loudly, and emptied the glass.

He hunched deeper into the shock chair, resting. "I'll be glad when it's over, Dillman. Really glad."

"Do you mean that, sir?"

"Hell yes, I mean it. In this business you've got to be tough. But I'll be damned if a man can go on kicking people around all the time. Someplace, he's got to stop. Well, this trip'll make my pile and I can stop. Got a job waiting, shuttling passengers to the Temple Ruins west of Red Sands of Mars."

"This isn't any party," Dillman admitted. "Slavery's a funny thing. I thought it went out a long time back, but everybody on Earth is making such mental advances..." he pointed at his skull and grinned wryly "...that they just haven't got any time to do any real work. And of course, these poor wastrels we've got on board aren't really human beings. How do they make them,

Cap?"

Caffrey shrugged. "God knows. The Globulars on Centauri Four turn them out by the hundreds. Almost as good as human beings.

They have kids, they get sick, they get mad, and they don't mind working. They don't know what else to do." He sighed, watching the circle of Mars beginning to grow big and bloated and red beyond the window. "Although it's one hell of a job to put muscle on them."

Dillman poured out some more liquor and raised his glass. His eyes were bits of hard rock. "Here's to the last trip, Cap. And I only hope the big boys of Workers, Incorporated, give me this ship."

Caffrey nodded and drank.

A green sign flashed over a bank of machinery. END OF EXERCISE PERIOD, it blinked, END OF EXERCISE PERIOD, END OF...

Rising, Caffrey walked to the machinery, pulled a large leather-handled switch. He visualized with pleasure the great doors opening, and the androids, the artificial humans; stumbling back into the dim stinking holds to wait quietly on the last stage of the trip before the chains closed on them. Caffrey laughed out loud.

"Dirty joke?" Dillman asked, faintly anxious.

"No. Just thinking about what I'll get paid. Two thousand solars. Why man, that's enough to live on for years! Plenty of wine, and an easy job, and women, bless 'em."

Dillman started to reply when the com system rattled. The big man moved to the machine and pressed the button.

"Caffrey, bridge," he growled. "What the hell is..."

A quiet voice cut him off, deadly, precise like a small knife slicing into him. "Captain, this is Doc. I'm down in the android hold. You'd better come right away."

"Doc," Caffrey began, but the machine clicked off. He slammed it with his fists. "Doc, damn it, Doc..." There was only the faraway rumble of the ship's great iron heart.

He swung around, heading for the door.

"Come on," he said quickly. "Nothing's going to happen. Not on this run. Nothing…"

They ran through the halls under the blue lights, clambered down the ladders, ran through more halls.

And then they stood in front of the big black door. Caffrey turned the wheel, slowly at first, and then faster, until it spun and blurred into invisibility. He stepped back; the doors opened.

THE hold was dark and musty. In the tiers of bunks, the androids huddled like not-quite-black shadows. They said nothing.

They watched. There was only a smell of antiseptic in the air, healthful, clean and rotten all at the same time.

Caffrey and Dillman moved through the endless rows of bunks. Farther down, Caffrey could see Doc crouching over a low bunk, his cigarette lighter aflame. He knelt there, a small bulbous gnome of a man, with weary defeated eyes and thin hair lying over his skull. An android boy of about seven years lay on the bunk.

Doc looked up as they stepped up to him.

His face was filled with the weariness of his eyes, with too many years and too much that was wrong.

"Well," said Caffrey, watching him. Doc's lighter jumped and flared bright when he spoke.

"The boy is sick," Doc said. "Very sick."

Caffrey clicked his fingernails together. "Did you call me down here for that?" There was a restless stirring from the bunks.

"Certainly," Doc replied. "It might be dangerous"

"What the hell's the matter with him?"

Doc shrugged. "I don't know. How do I know what diseases androids get? Don't you understand what this could mean?"

"No," said Caffrey, "I don't." His voice hardened. "I'm going back up to the chart room. We dock on Mars in a few hours."

Doc sighed and lifted his misshapen body. "All right." He turned to a woman near the bed. The woman's eyes were liquid and full of hurt. "I can't do anything," Doc said. "I don't know what's the matter with him." Caffrey felt stupid, seeing sorrow expressed for a woman who wasn't even human. Doc snapped his lighter closed and the circle of fire was gone. Caffrey breathed easily.

"It's too damned dark," Dillman whispered as they moved toward the door. He stumbled against a bunk and swore.

"Keep quiet," Doc said very softly. "Just you keep quiet."

Caffrey closed the black door and passed out cigarettes. The smoke whirled up to the ventilators like a dancing blue dragon. "Doc," he said, trying to control his anger, "I'd like to know why you're getting so excited."

"This is the first time I've seen disease in an android," the little man replied. "I don't know whether the disease is harmful to them or not. I mean seriously harmful. But remember what Terran scarlet fever did on Antares second. We've taken care of scarlet fever. It isn't fatal to us. But remember what it did to the people on Antares second."

"Yeah," said Dillman, leaning against the wall and covering his eyes.

Caffrey remembered too; the bodies and the fine yellow buildings and the rot and the inability to stop the corruption. The system had known panic.

"I see," he said. "You think whatever's wrong with that kid, even though it might not bother them much, might…kill us? Is that it?"

"Yes," said Doc. He blew out some smoke.

Caffrey grabbed his arm. "Nothing's going to happen. This cargo is going to Mars nothing's going to happen. I've worked for this a long time. Understand? No sick kid is going to keep me from landing on Mars."

"You're the captain," said Doc. He shambled off down the corridor, trailing a worm of blue smoke in the air behind him. He rounded a corner out of sight, small and gnarled and tired of arguing. The last of the smoke vanished into the ventilators.

Dillman laughed gratingly with effort. "Let's go get the rest of that bottle, Cap."

"Sure," said Caffrey.

They were three hours out from Mars when the com system came to life again. Caffrey jumped up out of the shock chair and jabbed the switch. A nervous, excited voice came screeching at him.

"Skolnik, Captain."

"What's wrong?"

"It's Doc. He's on the floor of his cabin. He's...I..."

"Speak up, man!" Caffrey yelled.

Skolnik's voice pulled itself back from shivering pieces and went on, "Doc's lying on the floor...and his voice is awful...and the muscles in his face and arms and all over him are jumping and...oh, Captain...

"Go on," Caffrey said savagely. "Go on!"

"...and he's screaming, Captain, and we can't stop him..."

Caffrey was out in the hall before the last syllable was uttered. The bulkheads spanged open as he kicked them. His feet slap-slapped frantically and when he was two sections away and one deck above Doc's quarters, he heard the screaming.

It rose and shrilled and howled and made him more afraid than he had ever been in his life.

The carefully acquired veneer of toughness shredded away like cheap cotton candy that was eaten at a Terran carnival and dissolved to nothing in the mouth.

The eighteen crewmen of the ship were in the hall, milling and twisting their caps in their hands. Skolnik stood with his back to the wall. He had vomited on the floor and now he was crying. Caffrey was sicker when he smelled the bitterness, but he shoved at the crewmen.

They stumbled against one another like dumb animals. Their faces belonged to little boys on dark nights when they walked home alone.

They seemed to resist Caffrey's efforts, and he clubbed at

them, the breath tearing in and out of his chest. Finally, he stood with his hands on the edge of the cabin door.

HIS hands had been sweating, but now he felt, actually felt, the wave of cold sweep through his fingers, up his arms.

Doc was on the floor, like Skolnik had said.

His scream made an endless mad tune above the engine rumble. His body was lifted from the floor, jerked, twisted, thrown back down again like some fantastic, jiggling marionette on strings.

"Doc," Caffrey called, "Doc, listen, it's me, Cap."

The screaming slobbered into nothing. Doc's hands clutched at the iron frame of his bunk. They held there while the rest of his body was convulsed and pulled into insane contortions.

"Infected," Doc said, forming his words into a shriek. "I got it from the child...we're all infected...all...we'll infect Mars...spread...spread...*spread*... "The last word went up and up like the ship's takeoff siren. Doc struggled to hold onto the bed but his body went jerking away across the floor.

Dillman peered over Caffrey's shoulder. The big man spoke very softly. "Go back to my cabin. Get my gun. Hurry."

Dillman hesitated, then ran. Caffrey stood fascinated watching the devil's dance of the diseased man. Finally, something cool and hard was placed in his hand. The scream tore at his eardrums.

Quickly he looked at the ceiling. He pushed the gun forward. He pulled the trigger several times. The shots roared and blended with the engine thunder. When the noise was gone, Caffrey realized that the screaming had stopped. He dropped the gun.

He turned around and closed the door of the cabin and locked it without once looking at Doc. Skolnik still sobbed over against the wall.

Rapidly, Caffrey explained what had happened in the android hold. The men stood, not looking at each other. They breathed loudly and the blue lights in the ceiling watched, emotionless.

Caffrey said, "We'll all be like that after a while."

"Maybe if we beam to Mars they'll know what to do," Dillman whispered. "Maybe we can get there in time, and maybe they can stop the disease."

Caffrey looked at him. "And maybe not."

He walked away. Dillman didn't follow. He walked back to the chart room and sat down in the shock chair. Beyond the port, Mars was large and waiting.

Caffrey thought seriously for the first time in many years. He wanted to get the ship to Mars. Maybe the doctors could help them. And maybe not.

They might infect others. The disease might spread, and if no one knew how to handle it...he didn't want to think about it.

Doc hadn't known what to do. Doc was a good man, medically. He had been a little run down, a little second-hand, because of his seedy deals and his need of money and his operations on women in dirty back alley rooms on a hundred worlds. But Doc couldn't stop it.

And sometime, Caffrey thought, alone and facing himself at last, a man has got to stop being tough. You can't live with yourself forever and be tough. Just once you've got to do something for your self-respect. He knew it, and all the cursing and shouting could not cover up the fact that he knew it.

There was a chance for them. But the chance might be deadly, more than deadly, to Sol's worlds. The androids didn't matter. They were pieces of metal and plastic and skin, constructed to get sick, but they didn't matter.

Caffrey laughed. *They didn't matter.* But they mattered when you thought of Doc being shaken to pieces in agony. Too perfectly made, they were. He laughed out loud at the tremendous mighty irony of the joke.

Dillman came in the door.

"What are we going to do, Captain?"

Caffrey stood up and sighed. He walked to the com system. He opened it. He spoke into it for a few moments. He shut it off. He turned to Dillman.

"That's what we're going to do," he said.

Dillman began to yell. He hit Caffrey, pummeled at him, screamed in fear. Caffrey had to knock him down on the floor and hit him with his cane. None of the other men gave him trouble.

Carefully, he moved to the course computer.

He made corrections in the directional tape. The ship began to groan. It swung into a new course. Caffrey took one final look at Mars, thinking of the quiet days, shuttling people to the Temple Ruins west of Red Sands, of the liquor and the warm, laughing women. But no more.

The sun lay dead ahead.

Caffrey sat down and poured himself a drink. Then he remembered something. If the disease hit him, he might alter the course.

He smashed the machinery, ripping it apart with his great hands, tearing it, so that the course could never be changed. Wires lay severed and bare all over the floor.

He picked up the bottle for another drink. The sun was a living ball of flame. He could not look at it.

The green sign went crazy. EXERCISE PERIOD, it blinked, EXERCISE...

Caffrey tried to throw the bottle at it. His hand twitched. The bottle fell to the floor and broke. Caffrey looked at his hands, at the hairs whitened with sunglow. The hand twitched again. Dillman stirred. His leg flapped once or twice.

Caffrey sat there while the heat began to melt the walls. He felt his body writhing, but it did not matter, in the heat. There was only a blinding whiteness all around. He thought about the androids. He thought about Skolnik. He thought, at last, about Mars.

He was still thinking about Mars when the ship fell into the burning maw of the sun.

THE END

Chicken

By
GREGORY LUCE

She was a gorgeous broad, as strippers go, not the kind of paunchy late-30s type you'd usually expect to find in a small, cheap nightclub out in the middle of nowhere. I took another drink. The cheap beer (it was dime beer night) trickled bitterly down my throat as my eyes followed her unflinchingly, pinpointing on every flesh-shaking, gyrating lust-bounce. She was easy on the eyes and just the thing I needed to help me relax a little before going back out on the road—two and a half more hours to Vegas. Then, for just a moment, something else caught my attention.

It was an alien monster.

Not a real monster of course, but it was there, nevertheless, hanging on the wall behind the stripper next to the fading Loni Anderson-in-bikini pin-up. It was obviously a poster from some crummy old sci-fi movie that I'd never bothered to catch on late night TV. There was a placard hanging beneath it. I strained to make out the inscription on it.

It read: "Welcome to the Alien's Rest."

Just then a rapidly shaking dual image blocked my view. The sleazy dance music had reached a tinny crescendo, and the stripper—back in front of me on the bar-top—was bent over at the waist, shaking her goods in a frenzied, high-speed jiggle just inches away from my face. The place erupted into a burst of hoot-laden applause. I stuck the cigarette back in my mouth and followed suit, shouting out my approval through cigarette-clenched lips.

The dancer made her way off the bar into a back dressing room, only after she disappeared through a side door did the applause die down. I signaled the bartender for another drink.

"Another beer?" he asked.

"Sure. It tastes like crud, but for a dime who cares."

He laughed slightly under his breath and popped open another bottle. It had a white generic label with one big word on it: BEER. As he started to pour, my attention went back to the odd placard on the far wall. I looked at him inquisitively.

"That sign on the wall over there...'Alien's Rest'...what does it mean?"

"That's the nickname for this place," he answered without looking up. The last of the rotgut beer trickled out of the bottle, then his eyes glanced up at mine. "It's 'cause of all the sightings we have around here."

I killed my cigarette in a dirty ashtray. "Sightings?"

"Flying saucers, aliens, UFOs...you know."

"You're kidding me."

He leaned over and spoke softly, almost whispering, pointing his thumb toward the other side of the room. "See those servicemen over there?"

I looked over and saw three Air Force personnel sitting at a table in the far corner of the room, just on the other side of an ancient pool table.

"What about 'em?" I asked.

His voice got even lower. "They work at a top secret military base about thirty miles from here...right out in the middle of the desert. It's a big test area for all the new top secret experimental aircraft and weapons that our government keeps buildin' and buildin' and we keep shellin' out billions and billions for."

"What does that have to do with UFOs?"

"Well that's just it. Nobody seems to know for sure...about the sightings I mean. We have a ton of 'em, but nobody seems to agree on just what it is we're all seein'."

I tipped my head back and got a perplexed look on my face. "Explain it to me."

"Some people say it's all alien hogwash...that it's nothin' but high-tech aircraft sightings...nothin' but a bunch of experimental stuff we put up there ourselves."

I shrugged my shoulders. "I guess that makes sense."

"Yeah, but it might make even *more* sense that it's aliens that we're seein'."

"How do you figure?"

"Well...think about it. If you were an alien civilization observing intelligent life on another planet, wouldn't you want to know everything about their science and technology? Especially in the area of flight and weapons development?" He carefully dropped my empty beer bottle into a small container below the bar. "Now don't get me wrong. I'm not saying every light we see in the night sky around here is from planet Mars or wherever. Certainly a lot of 'em have to be our stuff...sent up from Area 51 and S-4 and places like that. But some of 'em..." he leaned in real close, right into my face, "...some of 'em have gotta be from somewhere else." His index finger shot upward. "From *up there* somewhere. They're watchin' us...seein' what we're doin'...seein' what we're developing...seein' if we're any threat to 'em." He picked up a wet beer glass and started drying it. "Leastwise that's how I've got it figured."

I nodded in polite agreement, and for the next few minutes I listened to more of his extraterrestrial wisdom. The guy was obviously a UFO nut, but it probably kept him from going stir-crazy living in an out-of-the-way hole like this.

I looked down at my glass, it was almost empty. I raised it chin-high and held it there for a second or two.

"Here's to a night-time drive through the desert."

The bartender grabbed an empty shot glass and clinked glasses. Then I downed the last swallow. I smiled, left a buck on the counter, and headed for the door. Stepping outside, I glanced at my watch: It was nearly 1:00 a.m.

CHICKEN

The moonlit high desert was breathtaking. It was warm, too—a perfect night for driving. If I pushed it, I could probably be in Vegas in two hours. I pulled out my keys, sauntered over into the parking lot, stopped, and got a big smile on my face. There was a classic car sitting on the far side of the lot; its smooth surface glimmered in the moonlight.

It was my '57 Corvette.

Somehow it looked more stunning in the pale light of the moon. I stood staring in admiration for a few moments. It was one piece of beautiful machinery, a cherry rod if there ever was one. Sadly, we were soon to part company, or so was my plan. I needed the cash, needed it badly. I had a spot reserved at the big car show in Vegas the next day. A '57 soft-top would fetch a great price—15, 20, maybe as much as 25 grand. Not that I wanted to sell the car of my dreams, but divorces can be like that. And mine had been ugly, *very* ugly. Between child support and attorney's fees I was pretty well tapped. Jenny had gotten almost everything: the house, the kids, the furniture—she even managed to snag the vacuum cleaner and my *Beatles '65* album (She denied taking the latter, but I caught her humming *I Feel Fine* at the attorney's office one day). However, the one thing she hadn't gotten was the Vette. No. That was mine, at least for the time being. One last drive through the night air with the top down.

I slid behind the wheel and turned the key. The sound of the engine roaring to life cut loudly through the cooling atmosphere of the desert. I pulled out onto the highway. It was one of those ancient, narrow two-lane affairs, dotted here and there with equally antiquated road signs, some of which were scarred with rusted holes from shotgun pellets. There were no white border stripes, and the color of the asphalt wasn't much different than the color of the gravel shoulders, especially at night; so if you weren't paying attention and veered out of your lane, even just a little, you could find yourself spun out into a ditch. Fortunately, the roadway surface—for its age—was in remarkably good shape, largely because of the minuscule

34

number of vehicles that ever traversed it. In fact, at this time of night its long straight-aways made it a kind of shadowy, deserted racetrack, perfect for occasional drunken red-necks out to prove their manhood in weather-beaten pickup trucks with oversized wheels. It was a great road for the Vette, too. A great road for "punching it."

So I punched it.

The desert air rushed over the top of my head as I shot up the highway. Driving with the top down was an exhilarating feeling, no matter how many times I'd done it. I reached over and turned on the radio. A 50-thousand watt oldies station from southern Cal came booming in over the speaker. I knew most of the songs and started mouthing the words, pretending I was Ricky Nelson or Jerry Lee Lewis up in front of 10-thousand screaming fans. It was a nice little make-believe game I played whenever I was in the Vette by myself, especially on long road trips—a fantasy ego trip for an aging baby boomer. It also kept me from thinking too much about Jenny and the kids.

I was cruising along at about 70 mph, maybe half an hour from my final cheap beer when I saw it. At that moment I was thinking about that awful day when Jenny had walked in on Charlene and me in the camper. I remembered that awful wailing sound she had made as she ran crying back to the house in disbelief; but a gleaming pinpoint of light caught my attention and brought me back to reality. I thought it was a planet at first, a brilliant light in the distance mixed in with all the other heavenly bodies that shone so clearly through the thin air above the high desert. It was big, and it was bright, hanging there above the horizon, pretty much straight ahead, maybe a little to the left—probably Jupiter or Mars. I squinted at it a little, then drifted back to thoughts of Jenny. I'd been such a heel. Why couldn't I own up to the louse I'd been and ask her for forgiveness.

Then I noticed something different.

The light was still ahead, still shining brightly in the heavens, but now to the right. I was a little perplexed at first. I even turned my head to see if the road had curved slightly, causing the light's position to change. It hadn't. A long trail of gray asphalt lay in a straight line, fading in the pale distance to the rear of the Vette. I turned back around and stared real hard at the light. It was moving all right, slowly to the west. I eased back on the throttle and leaned forward. Must be a jet, I thought. No big deal. Then it did something that startled me. After moving slowly and steadily to the right, it suddenly made an abrupt right-angle turn and went straight down, plummeting toward the Earth at an increased speed. I lost sight of it as it dropped below a distant rise.

"What in the world..." I muttered.

My thoughts immediately flew back to the bartender at the cheap nightclub and all the extraterrestrial insight he had spouted to me. A light bulb of realization popped on over my head.

It's a spaceship...an alien spaceship!

I felt a slight rush of adrenaline and my foot instinctively pressed down harder on the gas pedal. A moment later I eased it back and shook my head in self-disdain, a half-smile on my face.

You idiot. It's nothing but some new-fangled military jet.

As my bartender buddy had also said, it was probably some piece of test aircraft the Air Force was trying out. Probably up from Area 51 or some other site on the Nellis Air Force Range. I settled back and turned up the oldies station. A minute later I was thinking about Jenny again. The highway shifted up hill.

Traveling Nevada's high desert takes you through a long series of desolate, spacious valleys separated by rises, sometimes steep grades. I was just coming to the top of the next grade when I heard a dull roar. An instant later the noise was gone. I looked up to see if a jet had passed overhead. There was nothing there. I came over the crest of the grade and started a steep descent into the next valley. The road got curvy at this point, twisting its way through a series of tall, rocky bluffs as it made its way toward the valley floor. I was approaching the last big curve just ahead of the next long straightaway. The dull roar sounded again. I came around the bluff and suddenly there it was, hovering a few hundred feet in front of me not more than two or three feet above the highway, all lit up like a Christmas tree.

It was a flying saucer.

Every muscle in my body tightened, but instead of hitting the brakes, my foot habitually pressed down on the gas pedal (it was the '60s hot rodder in me). The Vette shot ahead, straight for the UFO. It's funny what you do in bizarre situations like these, and I actually started honking the horn as I streaked toward it. Then I realized what I was about to do...suicide...my beloved Corvette was about to smack broadside into a UFO. I slammed on the brakes and started shouting.

"Get out of the way. Get out of the way! GET OUT OF THE WAY!"

The Vette went into a skid and I closed my eyes. However, the saucer rose up a few feet and we went skidding straight under it, slicing off onto the right shoulder. When the car hit the gravel it spun around. Rocks went flying everywhere. Amazingly, we did a complete 360 and settled to a stop. A shower of gravel came down on top of my prize vehicle. I sat there in shock, covered with pebbles. Chuck Berry was singing *Almost Grown* over the oldies station in the background. I looked over my shoulder and recoiled in astonishment.

The spacecraft was landing next to the Vette.

There were some dull scraping and clunking noises as the saucer hit the surface just to the rear of the car. It was the most extraordinary sight imaginable. I actually slapped the side of my face to make sure I wasn't hallucinating. This was a flying saucer, a real flying saucer, straddling the highway and the shoulder not five feet from my car. It was small, maybe 12 feet wide and about five feet high. There were brilliant white lights all the way around the outer edge. A dark blue light pulsated from the ship's rounded top and two smaller ones were blinking rapidly on its underbelly. Four small mechanical legs extended out from the main body, gripping the surface onto which the craft had slowly settled, all the time there was a dull whirring noise, undoubtedly the ship's engine.

I was petrified, scared to death. *Not real, not real, not real— can't be happening!* I closed my eyes and started counting, hoping it was all a bizarre hallucination. When I got to ten I opened them. The saucer was still there.

I took a deep breath and looked around me. Even in the dim light I could tell the Vette was a mess. I always left the ashtray open, so cigarette butts and ashes had gone flying everywhere. One butt had actually hit me in the eye. Gravel sprayed everywhere, too. The hood and interior were covered with it. I knew what it meant, too—scratches all over the paint job, little tiny scratches everywhere, there had to be. Through the terror of the moment I was suddenly angry. I could probably kiss five thousand off my asking price, maybe more, a classic Vette with a butchered paint job. No one would pay top dollar for a crippled cherry like that and no amount of buffing was going to make it right. It was going to need a full restorative paint job—again. It wouldn't be cheap, either. What was I going to tell my $200-an-hour divorce attorney who still had several thousand dollars in legal fees coming? For just an instant my mind went back to the divorce.

Dammit Jenny, why couldn't you have given me another chance?

Then something started happening on the saucer that distracted my rising anger. It was just a noise at first, the smooth sound of polished metal sliding over polished metal. I looked closer and saw a small, circular portal opening on the upper surface of the spacecraft, down a bit from its rounded top. I craned my neck up to see it better. A flash of movement caught my eye, just below the lip of the portal.

There was something alive inside, just out of sight.

I heard what sounded vaguely like a button clicking. A whirring noise followed; I almost cried out. Rising up in front of me through the portal was the head and upper torso of a very small alien being. The escalating platform it was standing on stopped before its entire body was visible.

"Holy sweet mother of…" I whispered under my breath. It was the ugliest damn thing I had ever seen.

There were four arms hanging from the middle of a weird spiral-shaped torso. I couldn't see what kind of legs were supporting it (or how many for that matter), but it didn't appear to be over a foot or two in height. A rapid chattering noise came out of an orifice in the middle of its triangular-shaped head. I nearly laughed it sounded so funny. It kept saying the same thing over and over, all the while moving one of its four arms in what appeared to be a jerky, beckoning wave. I listened closely, but it didn't make any sense—pure gibberish. Then its speech pattern slowed. I jerked with surprise as I realized the sounds now had a familiar ring, it was trying to communicate with me in English. I strained to make out the words, which were being repeated over and over, slower and slower, until I was finally able to understand them.

"Pleased to meet you."

This time I did laugh out loud. Its wiggly arm kept beckoning to me in a spasmodic manner, then two of its many tiny fingers raised up in what seemed to be roughly the shape of a V. I couldn't be sure, and it seemed ridiculous, but it appeared the bizarre visitor from another world was flashing me the peace sign.

"Child of the 60s?" I asked, then laughed even louder.

There I was, sitting in a '57 Chevrolet Corvette in the middle of the high desert after midnight with a bizarre-looking alien trying to strike up an extraterrestrial friendship. I laughed for a few more seconds before my mirth turned back to anger. I glanced back at the hood: The paint job was ruined. Selling the Vette at the car show was going to be nearly impossible and my legal fees would probably drive me into bankruptcy, all because a miniature alien had wanted to come down and chat for a while.

"Take your peace sign and shove it, you stupid, dumb son of an alien bitch!"

I raised my fist in defiance and flipped up my middle finger. The alien got a strange look on its face, as though it fully understood the meaning of my obscene gesture and wasn't too pleased. I didn't care, though. I turned the key, dropped it into first, and peeled out, and I mean *peeled* out—my foot went all the way to the floor. A shower of gravel flew from the rear of the Vette and cascaded up over the surface of the saucer. I knew the alien got a face-full, because it squealed in obvious pain. I looked behind me; the creature had all four of its hands in front of its face.

"Serves you right...Asshole!"

The Vette lurched back onto the pavement and we sailed down the highway. There was still gravel all over the interior; I brushed some of it off me. I hadn't noticed before, but the oldies station was still blaring away. The speedometer hit 90 right as Jackie Wilson went into the last chorus of *Lonely Teardrops*. I looked back as I started up the next rise: The saucer was still there, sitting on the edge of the roadway. The Vette sailed over the crest and started down into the next valley; the spacecraft disappeared from view.

"Hallelujah."

I was a nervous wreck for the next 10 minutes or so. A car passed me coming the opposite direction and I thought about flashing my brights and flagging them down; but even if they stopped, what the hell was I going to tell them, "Watch out for the midget alien down the road?" They wouldn't believe me and they'd find out for themselves soon enough, anyway.

My right hand patted the steering wheel. "Just get me to Vegas."

A few more minutes went by and I started to calm down a bit. The anger remained, though. In fact, the calmer I got the more I seethed about what had happened. It all brought my thoughts back to Jenny. *Quit being a stubborn SOB and tell her you're sorry...ask her for another chance...throw yourself at her feet and beg for mercy.* I shook my head. *Quit torturing yourself.*

My thoughts turned to the alien. What was I going to do? Should I tell the police? The military? Maybe I should just keep my mouth shut. Then something caught my attention.

There was a light moving across the western sky.

I could feel my heart speed up. It was the saucer again, traveling along at a slow speed, maybe a couple of miles away, a few hundred feet off the ground. My speed slowed as my head craned right to follow its motion. It seemed to be paralleling my course. I pulled the Vette over to the side of the road and stopped. The saucer did the same, hanging over the desert floor in the distance, waiting for my next move. I pulled back onto the highway and gradually increased speed. The saucer did likewise, building its speed, still paralleling me to the right. This went on for another minute or two, then it changed course and accelerated.

It was heading toward the highway.

It got brighter and brighter as it closed the distance. I immediately sped up. It was coming in at an angled descent that appeared to be on a collision course with the Vette.

"Aw crud," I muttered to myself. Then I floored it.

It was close enough now that I could see the individual lights on its metallic surface. Suddenly there was a burst of acceleration and the spacecraft streaked over the top of the Vette at an incredible speed. I didn't even have time to duck. It came around in front of me again and climbed to a higher elevation. The saucer was now directly over the highway in front of me, matching my speed and traveling in the same direction.

The next thing that happened made my blood freeze. As the saucer climbed back into the sky, the volume of the oldies station, which was still booming away, gradually diminished. As Aretha Franklin's voice faded to nothingness, a new sound came in, getting louder and louder. It was the chattering voice of the alien, and it was saying the same thing over and over at high speed. Then, as before, the sound slowed, like a 33-and-a-half rpm record being played back at 78 and then gradually being brought back to normal speed. The alien gibberish transformed into English once more.

"So you think you have a fast automobile?"

With that, the alien reversed engine and cut straight back at me, zooming over the top of the Vette so close I could feel a strong gust of wind. I hit the brakes momentarily, then sped up. The saucer continued to cat-and-mouse me for the next several minutes. It buzzed me from the left, then from the right. What made me almost swerve into the ditch though, was when it buzzed me from the rear. I started screaming obscenities on its next pass. Another grade was approaching. As I started climbing, the saucer disappeared. I slowed up a little. My head was bobbing every which way, looking over the heavens in search of my extra-terrestrial harasser. The alien was no where in sight, though. I breathed a sigh of relief; for a minute I thought I might be free of him.

I whispered to myself sarcastically, "Nothing like a nice, peaceful, relaxing drive through the desert."

When I came down into the next straightaway my hands gripped the steering wheel tightly. There was a bright light, maybe two or three miles in the distance, hovering just above the surface of the highway. The alien was back.

"Dammit! What the hell do you want?" I shouted. My foot went to the brake. "No more games." With that, I pulled over to the side of the road and stopped. The saucer was just hanging there, waiting. It was like an extraterrestrial stare-down contest. Then a dim light flashed on the surface of the spacecraft and something streaked out of it, straight up into the night sky. Whatever it was appeared to be quite small. It made a couple circles above the saucer, then came straight toward me. My heart started pounding and a surge of blood rushed through me.

It's a bomb...an alien bomb!

I reached down and started the engine, but the small streaking object slowed up. It descended slowly and began circling a few yards above the Vette. I crouched down in my seat and closed my eyes, preparing for the worst. I figured an explosion was imminent. Nothing happened, though, and after a few moments I opened my eyes and looked up. Circling just above me was some kind of probe, completely round and about the size of a basketball. It had a number of soft blue lights polka-dotting its metallic surface.

I yelled at it. "What do you want!?"

It moved away, maybe twenty yards or so, behind the Vette. I eased my foot down on the gas pedal and crept back onto the highway.

Then it started shooting power beams at me.

That's right...power beams. That's the only way I can describe them. Little streaks of red light. They were cascading out of the probe in rapid-fire succession, dozens of beams per second. As they peppered the ground they caused little mini-explosions; the noise was deafening. The overall pattern of the blasts hitting the ground was like a big horseshoe. The probe, still blasting away, gained speed and moved closer to my slow moving Vette. I punched it. For a moment I left the probe to the rear, but it soon accelerated and moved up right behind me. It was getting closer and closer, still firing away with its power beams, still in a dazzling horseshoe pattern. I looked ahead: The saucer was still hovering above the highway in front of me, not more than two miles away.

The probe got right up on my rear end. The umbrella of power beams actually encircled the rear and sides of the Vette, not more than six feet away on any side. I sped up some more—the speedometer hit 90. The probe still hung tightly to the rear. I looked directly ahead of me. The saucer lay in my path, about a mile or so down the road. I gasped as I realized what was happening.

The saucer was now moving toward me.

It was no longer hovering in one spot. Instead, it was streaking toward me at a high speed, not more than a foot or two above the roadway. We would collide in a matter of moments. A wave of panic shot through me. I couldn't slow down or veer off, the umbrella of power beams would fry me. I realized what was going on. I was being herded...herded into a collision with an extraterrestrial spacecraft. I gripped the wheel hard and tried to ease off on my speed, but as I did the power beams got nearer and nearer. My foot pressed back down on the throttle. The alien had no intention of letting me get out of its way. Impact was only seconds away. Then, as the panic of an impending, horrible death was overtaking me, the power beams suddenly disappeared.

The probe was gone!

The saucer loomed larger and larger in front of me. I jerked the wheel and hit the brakes. The Vette plowed off onto the shoulder of the road, barely missing the passing spacecraft. Gravel went flying everywhere again as the Vette slid to a stop. My voice reverberated loudly through the desert night air as I let loose with a fusillade of obscenities.

Once again the oldies station began to fade. The familiar chattering noise of the alien swelled in once more. It was an unintelligible phrase being said over and over again at high speed. As it gradually slowed, the strange sounding English put an expression of incredulity on my face...

"What's the matter...chicken?"

Before I could react, the flashing lights of the saucer caught my attention. I looked to the rear and saw it descending slowly toward the highway surface. It came within a few feet of the asphalt and stopped, hovering motionlessly above the highway. After a few seconds I could see the circular portal opening up, but this time only part of the alien's body reappeared. It was a skinny arm with a rubbery-looking hand on top. I couldn't tell how many fingers were on the hand because it appeared to have them all clinched into a tiny fist, all save one, one right in the middle that was extended straight up in the air.

The alien was flipping me off.

I started laughing like lunatics in nuthouses sometimes do. The fist was rocking gently, back and forth. This must have gone on for at least half a minute or more before I got control of myself and eased the Vette back out on the roadway. This time I didn't peel out. This time I didn't flip him off. Even though my whole body was quaking from shock and fear, I managed to turn my head and shout back at the saucer.

"I'm sorry!"

I didn't know if an apology would do any good at this point, but I figured it was worth a try, anything to get me out of this nightmare. I slowly pressed down on the accelerator as we moved away from the alien ship, not too fast, but at a leisurely pace. The saucer was still sitting there, the tiny hand still waving back and forth. *Take your time...don't rush, don't rush...don't do anything sudden.* I must have been about a mile down the road before I even got it up to 40. *No hurry...plenty of time. Don't give him a reason to chase you.* I took another glance over my shoulder: The saucer was gone. I felt another adrenaline rush. My eyes frantically searched the night skies, my head jerking spastically in every direction. The spacecraft was nowhere to be seen.

Where did he go?

There was a long, fairly straight grade in front of me, so I decided to punch it. Maybe the alien had had enough fun with me, maybe it was bored; but I wasn't going to stick around to find out. I flew up the grade at 80 miles an hour. I became dimly aware of the oldies station again. The lyrics to *Catch Us if You Can* by the Dave Clark Five were suddenly ripe with black humor. The side of my mouth winced a painful, half-smile. I was nearing the top of the grade, but I refused to slow up. We went flying over the crest at 85 miles an hour. I didn't see the curve on the other side until it was almost too late. I jerked the wheel hard to stay on the road. I overcompensated and swerved into the other lane.

Then I saw the headlights of a truck directly in front of me.

I swerved again and hit the brakes at the same time. The truck—a tractor and semitrailer—did likewise, blasting its air horn long and loud. Its lights were on bright, and I could see the two rows of yellow marker lights on either side of the air horn. I was almost blinded. Luckily, it had been crawling up the other side of the grade at a leisurely pace, I cranked the wheel hard and swerved off onto the right shoulder of the road as the enormous, lumbering vehicle missed the Vette by inches. For the third time that night, the Vette came sliding to a stop in a shower of gravel. This time the engine stalled. The semi slowed and started pulling off to the side of the road.

"This is *not* funny anymore!" I yelled. My eyes darted everywhere, looking for my alien pursuer. The spacecraft was still nowhere to be seen, though, having seemingly disappeared into the heavens. Then a voice from behind caught my attention.

"Damn, mister! Are you okay?"

I turned around to see the truck driver, obviously concerned, jogging down the highway toward me. The truck itself had come to a stop on the other shoulder, not far back up the road. In the bright moonlight I could tell the driver was a tall, skinny guy, running with a bit of a limp. He appeared to be wearing a baggy, over-sized jacket and some kind of a sportsman's cap that was pushed way back on his head. I thought it was going to fall off as he bounced down the road in my direction.

I called out to him. "Did you see it? Did you see that damned thing?"

"Did I see wha—" his voice cut off and he abruptly stopped in his tracks. There was a dull roar from behind me. Before I could even glance around, the saucer rushed over my head and came to a mid-air stop, hovering about 40 feet off the ground, maybe ten yards up the road between the Vette and the truck. The driver stood there for a second, then screamed like a baby. He turned and ran. His foot must have hit a broken spot on the edge of the pavement, because his whole body went sprawling onto the shoulder. He screamed hysterically. As he got back up he reached down and grabbed a small handful of loose gravel and threw it at the saucer. The pebbles sailed up and fell harmlessly to the ground, missing the saucer completely. He looked so pathetic throwing them I would have almost laughed had I not been so petrified myself. As the driver climbed back into the cab of the truck, I put the Vette into neutral and turned the key. It roared back to life. I took one last glance over my shoulder and saw the truck driver climbing back out of the cab. A rifle was in his hands.

"What are you doing?" I yelled at him.

I couldn't tell if it was a big hunting rifle or some kind of shot gun, but he stood there on the cab step and pointed it at the alien ship. I don't know what he thought he was going to do. Shoot down a flying saucer with a rifle? The guy was nuts.

A shot rang out; I heard a loud pinging noise off the side of the spacecraft. What happened next jarred me so much I thought I was going to black out. There was a high-pitched squeal and a brilliant, almost blinding flash of light.

A massive force beam shot out of the saucer.

In the same instant, the truck and its driver were literally blown to smithereens. The fireball was enormous; I threw my hands over my face. A split second later, a shock wave sent me sprawling over in the seat as the Vette rocked back and forth from the concussion. Flaming debris went sailing up into the sky, only to come showering back down onto the desert floor moments later. A large chunk of burning tire landed with a loud thump just a few feet from the rear of the Vette. Now I was the one screaming.

In spite of the blast, the Vette's engine was still running. I punched my foot down on the gas pedal as hard as I could. The Vette leaped off the shoulder and went shooting down the lonely desert highway, a swath of burning wreckage to the rear. I was descending into a long, spacious valley surrounded by jagged peaks whose magnificent features were reduced to inky silhouettes by the brilliant light of the moon above. The road ahead was a straight shot for several miles. It faded into dim nothingness toward the far end of the valley. The speedometer hit 80, 90, then 100.

The rush of the night air over the open Vette was thunderous, but I could still hear the booming music of the oldies station cutting through. It was playing some rock and roll oldie I'd never heard before, but it soon faded. That creepy, rapid fire alien chatter swelled up and drowned out the music again, high speed nonsense at first, then slowing into clear English, the same six words over and over...

"Let's see if you're still chicken..."

As fearful as I was, this really got under my skin. I had beaten the best street rodders of my time, and no tiny alien was going to get the best of me. I felt that old "I've-got-the-top-rod-on-this-street" attitude surging up inside. Something flickered in the distance. I saw a light plummeting from the heavens a few miles ahead of me. The saucer was descending back to the highway. I pushed my speed up to 105. Suddenly explosions surrounded the rear and sides of the Vette.

The probe had returned.

The umbrella of power beams was there again, driving me straight into a high-speed showdown with the saucer ahead. I didn't care, though.

"Can you take what you dish out?" I called out to the saucer in the distance.

A strategy then occurred to me. I started veering from side to side. The probe kept tight on my rear. I wanted it to keep on my tail. I wanted it to stay with me as long as possible, to the last possible second. The saucer was dead ahead, maybe a foot or two above the road, coming toward me at a tremendous rate of speed, even faster than before. It was going to be close, but I wanted it to end, one way or another.

I screamed at the approaching spacecraft. "You picked the wrong Vette to rumble with!" I must have sounded like an idiot.

I was still steering slightly from side to side. The probe followed relentlessly while the saucer streaked toward me, getting bigger and bigger. The power beams came within inches of the Vette. The probe was hanging in there, staying on my tail much longer this time.

Stay with me...just another second or two.

The saucer was only an instant away before the probe finally started to break off. At that moment I slammed on the brakes as hard as possible. I thought my foot might go right through the floor. As the brakes took hold, the Vette went into a sideways skid, like the head of an old Hoover vacuum cleaner plowing its way down a long carpet of gray asphalt. I was terrified that the car might go into a roll, but it didn't. The moonlit eastern desert skyline lay peacefully in my field of vision, glaringly accented by the sound of rubber screaming against pavement. I was going to broadside the saucer. There was a rush of hot air and lights flashed inches above me. A thunderous clap of metal slamming into metal pierced my ears. My strategy had worked.

The saucer had pulled up and collided with the probe!

It was more than I could have hoped for. As the Vette came sliding to a stop, I heard a terrific thud off to the west side of the road, maybe fifty yards or so. I looked over.

The probe had crashed into the desert floor!

I was a little disoriented, and it was a miracle the Vette hadn't rolled. Then I saw something that made me cry out in astonishment. Veering off to the eastern side of the highway was the alien spacecraft. It was cutting through the air a few dozen yards above the desert floor, locked in a continual corkscrew, completely out of control. A moment later it slammed into the desert surface, sand and sagebrush flying everywhere. I sat there in stunned silence for a moment or two.

Then I went crazy.

I let out a victory scream that must have been heard in Carson City. I was laughing; I was crying; and all the while I kept on screaming at the top of my lungs. I was bouncing up and down in the seat of the Vette, hurling every obscenity known to man at my fallen alien predator. I went from total terror to total exhilaration. It was the greatest rush you could imagine.

For a second or two I actually thought about climbing out of the car and checking out the crash sight. What a great way to win Jenny and the kids back. You know, be a hero and all that. *Let's kick some alien butt.* I could even grab an extraterrestrial souvenir or two.

I must have been nuts.

After a few moments, reason prevailed. *Just get back on the road and get the hell out of here.*

Then I heard something that startled me. Connie Francis was singing *Where the Boys Are* on the oldies station, but her lilting voice was fading slowly into the background as something else came in over the top of it.

It was the alien.

The high-speed chatter faded up over the music. The actual audio quality seemed more unusual this time, louder, like stereo or surround sound. Then I realized it wasn't coming from just the radio, but also from the desert, to the east. It was echoing across the sagebrush from the crippled alien spacecraft itself. It was the eeriest damned thing I had ever heard. The rapid-fire alien gibberish once again started to slow. I strained to make it out. However, this time there were no words to decipher. It was something far more chilling than any words could be, something that sent a cold feeling of raw terror through me more than anything else that night.

It was laughter.

A continual Ha Ha Ha Ha Ha pounded into my ears. It wasn't a natural laugh, but a forced, repetitive sound that you might expect from one who wasn't familiar with natural human sounds, and it made my skin crawl. I turned around and grabbed the wheel with both hands.

Punch it. Get out of here NOW.

I floored it and shot up the road at a tremendous speed. Within moments I had the speedometer near 100. I had to get out of this valley. It was another two, maybe three miles. That horrid laughter still blared out of the radio.

"Ha Ha Ha Ha Ha..."

I reached over and turned it off. I knew something awful was going to happen. The speedometer hit 115. The Vette had never been up that fast before, not with me at least. There had never been a need, not even in my street-rodder days. I thought the wind was going to blow the top of my head right off, but I kept the accelerator all the way down.

Gotta go faster...gotta go faster!

Although my thoughts were frantic, somehow they came back to Jenny.

Just let me get out of this. Let me get out of this and I'll make it up to you, Jenny. I'll make it up to you and the kids. I'll do whatever I can to make things right again.

I began climbing a long, gradual slope whose summit formed the far edge of the valley. Thank goodness it wasn't a steep, curvy grade. The road still continued pretty much in a straight line, bending only slightly to the left. I wouldn't even have to slow up. The needle on the speedometer was quivering just under 120. Something told me if I made it to the other side of the summit I'd be safe. I flipped the radio back on. The weird laughter still blared out of the speaker. I was near the top of the grade. Then the laughter stopped and the alien's tinny voice came in. Its words completely unnerved me.

"You have to hurry...run...run...run...ha, ha, ha, ha, ha..."

The laughter intensified and became even more chilling. I reached over and killed the radio. The speedometer said I was now going a little over 120. The rounded valley summit lay in front of me now, just seconds ahead. I prayed there weren't any sudden curves on the other side. Far away peaks rose up dimly in the distance as the highway leveled off at the summit then started a gradual downward course into the next valley. I was over the top. Still, nothing had happened. I didn't know what to expect, except that it was going to be bad. A Corvette-seeking missile perhaps? The one thing I did know was that I couldn't keep going at this tremendous speed. I'd eventually crash and burn if I didn't slow down. The road was heading into a long curve as we came down the other side, so I braked the Vette—gently—and brought us back down to 80. It seemed like we were crawling. I reached down and turned on the radio. The laugher was gone. There was nothing this time: no oldies station, no laughter, just the quiet sound of dead air. I turned the volume knob up all the way—still nothing.

Then an explosion of white noise blew out my speaker.

For a moment my hands left the wheel and instinctively reached up to cover my ears. I cried out in pain. At the same instant, the northern sky behind me went bright, all lit up like the dawn. A few seconds later the roar of an explosion reached my ears. My heart started to pound. It was obvious what had happened.

That crazy alien has blown himself sky high!

I knew what the laughter had meant now. The alien was trying to take me out along with him. He was trying to have one last laugh on me. My foot crushed down on the accelerator. I knew a blast wave was probably streaking up from behind. The speedometer leaped back over 100. In what I figured were my last moments on Earth, my thoughts came back to Jenny and the kids. I wanted desperately to live. I wanted just one more chance to prove myself. A blast wave was imminent, though. It would come barreling over the top of the summit like a giant steamroller. Joshua trees and Yucca plants would go flying into the air as they were disintegrated into a million tiny particles—I could just see it. I reached over and turned my review mirror up so I *wouldn't* see it. My foot was all the way to the floor. It's funny, when you get a car up that fast on a long stretch of road in the middle of the night, the broken line down the center of the pavement just melts into a solid, white blur. How fast did I get up to? I didn't even glance at the speedometer—125, maybe

130. I'll never know for sure. A lone chuckhole in the road would send me tumbling into oblivion.

After a few moments I turned the rearview mirror back down expecting to see a wall of death racing up on me, but the moonlit desert leading back toward the summit was still peaceful and undisturbed. The bright flash of light had faded and no blast wave was apparent. I didn't know how big or forceful the explosion had been. Perhaps it hadn't been powerful enough to reach beyond the summit. In fact, I didn't know absolutely for sure that the alien ship itself had even blown up. Perhaps there wasn't any real explosion at all. Maybe it was some kind of visual or electronic hoax—the alien's idea of a final practical joke. He might be soaring slowly over the desert in his injured ship, laughing at me riotously. I would probably never know for sure. But if there indeed had been some horrible force chasing me down, it never caught up to me. I had beaten it. After a few more minutes, I gradually brought the Vette back down to a sane speed. As I went over the next summit, I stared into the rearview mirror: only darkness and twilight were behind me.

You can't possibly imagine the feeling of relief that flooded over me. I slowed down a bit and looked over my shoulder. All I could see was a dark, peaceful sky filled with thousands of twinkling stars. At that moment I knew I was going to make it. It was over...*finally*. With that I pulled the Vette over and came to a complete stop. I wrapped my arms around the wheel, put my head down, and wept like a baby for half and hour.

What a night.

I cruised into Las Vegas about an hour later. I checked into a cheap motel and crashed for 18 hours, missing the first day of the car show. The TV and newspapers never said anything about an explosion in the desert or an incinerated truck. None of that mattered to me, though. What mattered were the things I learned that night. Like the end of a good sci-fi movie, I learned we aren't really alone and just how insignificant we can sometimes be. You could even say I learned some lessons in manners—the hard way. But as much as a man can ever be certain, I learned that night that Jenny was the one true love of my life. I knew that somehow I'd get her and the kids back. But I also learned the best friend I ever had was a '57 Vette...

and nothing would *ever* take her away from me.

THE END

The Two Sharp Edges

By
ALGIS BUDRYS

"We left when the war came; we went back to my father's birthplace. But when we went back, we had to go in a spaceship."

THE HILLS to which Henry Walters came in the Spring of 1965 were not like the gentle flatness of the land on which he had been born; the bite of the air was deeper than that to which he was accustomed, for this time of year. But he could feel the country—understand its mood and the reasons why the people who had lived in it had put their marks upon it as they had. The farmhouses and buildings were not in familiar, but in understandable shapes, and he knew the run of a furrow that takes the most growing room from a swelling hillside.

In the Spring of 1965, any man so fortunate was as close to home as he was free to hope. Henry Walters turned his worn old car down the narrow road to the village in the valley, found the local representative of the Office of Resettlement and Rehabilitation, and bought a farm with the land-credits in his mustering-out paybook. And for a year, through the needling Summer's heat, the smoky Fall and hearth-warmed Winter, Henry was perhaps closer to home than even R&R's envisioners had ever aspired.

IT WAS ANOTHER Spring, and the fields above the farmhouse were deep in twilit green. From where he was standing on the slope, Henry looked down on the red and dark purple-blue sky reflected on the pond in the hollow of the hill, and his thinning hair stirred to the breeze that rolled down the hillside and broke the pond's surface into a hundred thousand polychrome refractions.

A year had been enough to bring the untenanted land back from the blurring that years had brought to its face. Alone, be worked through daylight into night, the cough of his tractor's engine echoing back from the hills; and while the furrows stretched themselves into the soil, and the fences squared their sagging shoulders, he learned every lesson the farm could teach him. And now that the cycle had begun once more; each blade of grass was an old friend, come home from the Winter. Once again, the land was given life, and gave life in return.

The strangers drove into his yard, four of them, and got out of the car, standing in the uncertain tight group of unannounced trespassers on another man's property while they looked for him.

Henry walked down the hill toward them. They saw him before long, but did not wave or shout needless greetings at him. He might have stopped and waited for them to come to him, if they had acted impatient, but they stood quietly together, with their faces turned up at him as he came down the hill; and even while he was some distance away from them, there seemed to be a sort of gentle defensiveness about the four men.

Three of them were about the same age, all in their middle twenties. The fourth seemed to be as much again older than they. They were part of the same family, dark-eyed, and as thin as Henry himself; but even the three younger men had heavy tracks of silver through the dark hair along the sides of their heads. As he came up to them, he saw the indecision at their mouths and the uncertainty of their looks. He noticed, too, that their clothes were a little old-fashioned—prewar— but must have been kept carefully stored somewhere, for, even allowing for the superiority of material, they were remarkably little worn. Their car was a prewar model as well, just as most were, but someone had given it far better than average care.

"Good evening," Henry said.

The older man seemed to regard it almost as a direct observation, for he took a deep breath of the twilight breeze and let his glance touch the sky and fields.

"Good evening," he answered. He held out his hand. "My name is Harold Piper. These are my sons; David, Charles, and Edward. You are Mr. Walters?" The diffident, slightly embarrassed strain was in his voice, as well.

Each of the sons had nodded to his name, and Henry answered in kind. He shook Harold Piper's hand. "I'm Henry Walters. Pleased to meet you and your sons, Mr. Piper."

"I ought to explain," Piper said haltingly. "You see, this used to be my farm, before the war." His glance was on the fields again.

He looked back at Henry suddenly, as though guilty of theft. "We're not here to take it back," he said quickly. Henry twinged in inward sympathy at the hastiness of the man's explanation. It was a hard situation for a man to be in. He felt far from comfortable himself, and a selfish part of him wished that the man hadn't come. He could think of nothing to say in answer, and stood silently, waiting for Piper to go on.

"My wife and I and the boys left, when the war started. That made it public land." He looked at Henry's shirt, which might have simply been a garment bought in a surplus store, but wasn't. "You stayed, and whatever you did, you earned it." He looked up at the orchard, which Henry had carefully pruned and sprayed. "We inquired, down at the Rehabilitation office; they said you've only been here a year."

Henry nodded. "That's right. Just about an even year."

He wished he could think of something more to say, instead of standing here awkwardly in the yard, watching Piper struggle with his own words.

"You've taken good care of it," Piper said, becoming more and more obviously embarrassed.

"Look," Henry said, pushing the words out hastily, not sure if he was doing the right thing or not, "would you like to come inside for a while? I'm alone up here, but I can offer you something to drink, and a bite to eat."

THE OFFER seemed to embarrass Piper even more. His hands moved nervously over his coat pockets, fumbling at their contents until one of his sons reached forward, apologizing uncomfortably as his arm came between Piper and Henry, and gave his father a cigarette. Piper lit it after a number of ineffectual attempts with the lever of his lighter, and puffed rapidly and jerkily before he answered.

"Thank you. Thanks—that's very kind of you. But we ought to be on our way; we just drove up for a look at the place. You know how it is." He swept his guilty eyes over the land again. "We—we've got relatives in—" He stopped and looked at his sons, his eyes demanding support. "—New Haven. In New Haven." He stopped, and he and his sons shared the same uncomfortable look.

Henry took a deep breath, and was glad the twilight was at least deep enough to let him hope the pity in his eyes was shadowed. "Mr. Piper, excuse me, but I don't think you're going anywhere. I don't think you've got any relatives in New Haven. I don't think you've *got* anywhere to go, and I wish you'd at least stay and have something to eat."

He watched the truth reflect itself on the faces of the four men, and he hated what he'd done to their pride; but pride wasn't the most important thing any more—not in 1966— and a drink and a meal offered with an open hand were at least a sign to a man that he wasn't unwelcome everywhere.

Piper sighed. He gave up the struggle with his features, and his face, stripped of its mask, was somehow more serene and self-contained, "You're quite right, Mr. Walters," he said, the sigh still strong in his voice. He looked at his sons. "We'll stay, boys."

Henry looked at the three sons, and at their father. Something crawled through the short hair at the back of his neck. DP's shouldn't be speaking perfect American; they shouldn't be dressed in American clothes, and have American names. They weren't supposed to come to you, the usurper, and stand humiliated on land which had once been theirs, with a phantom woman, a wife and mother, who had left with them but had not returned save in the far corners of their hurt faces. Henry knew there was nothing he was expected to do. This land was his, now; and he himself had a lost home, and his own phantoms.

"Good. Let's get inside, then," he said hoarsely.

THEY ATE silently, sitting around the kitchen table. Henry had done the best he could with a pair of chickens and what he had in the springhouse, and he'd brought out the half-bottle of Four Roses he'd picked up on the outskirts of New York. But they ate without speaking, and Henry was glad of it.

He watched the Pipers slowly relax. Their movements lost their constrained stiffness, and their heads slowly rose from their first deliberate concentration on their plates. Henry could feel his own thinking unknot in response.

There wasn't anything he or the Pipers could do. The land was his; the government had given it to him in compensation for the years of war. The Pipers had abandoned it, and had no claim on it. It was a tough break for them, but it wasn't Henry's fault. This was his home, now, but if he'd had things the way he'd have liked them, the Pipers would still be here, all five of them, and he'd never have left New Jersey.

What he was saying, he realized, was that if he'd had things the way he wanted them, there wouldn't have been any war. That was all the Pipers were saying, too, with their wounded faces.

Finally, the last plate was pushed back, and Henry gathered up the dirty dishes hastily, wishing that nobody would say anything, hoping that when he turned around from the sink he would find the Pipers silently gone.

He turned around, and Harold Piper said, "That was a very good meal, Mr. Walters. Thanks you."

"Wasn't much," Henry answered. He was so preoccupied with his thoughts that he went on automatically. "The cooking really needs a woman's tou—"

He stood there stupidly, his mouth helpless and agape, his eyes remorselessly showing him the faces of the four Pipers. He took a deep breath finally, his face pale. "I'm sorry," he said. "Didn't think."

Piper smiled gently, his eyes dark but his face composed. "No. Mr. Walters," he said his voice steadier than Henry expected, "There's nothing for you to be sorry about. You're quite right. Any home needs a woman. Yours lacks one, and there is nothing more natural for you than to mention the fact." Something—but only the barest, most carefully controlled shadow of something—passed across his features and accentuated the darkness in his eyes. "Any other connotation is…irrelevant. A man should not go through life continually watching out for every stranger's toes. It makes for an erratic path."

Somehow, Henry's obvious embarrassment had put him on an even level with the Pipers. He felt the change in the atmosphere clearly, and was glad it had come, finally ending the intolerable strain. But he did not know exactly what to say in reply to Piper's last statement and he felt his hands twitch ineffectually.

Piper was getting up, his sons rising with him. "You've been very kind. It has been an awkward situation, through no fault of yours."

The iron control, which only the first impact of their return to the occupied farm could have broken as much as it had, kept Piper's face and voice locked in calmness. "Thank you for your hospitality; we'll be going."

HENRY LOOKED at the four men. The father's mask was mirrored by his sons. There was no hint on the worn faces that nothing waited for them but the unknown, and homelessness. And he remembered, sharply, that from the very first there had not been the slightest gesture or action on any of their parts to indicate that they were not on someone else's property. Even before they had seen him on the hillside, or known he was watching them, they had remembered that the farm was his, now, and that his courtesy was all that gave them any right to be here.

"Wait—look," he blurted. "You don't have to go yet. It's night; you haven't got any place to stay, and you know you won't find one. There's room for you here." He almost added, "You know that," and stopped himself barely in time.

The pride rose in Piper's expression. "Thank you. That's very generous of you, but—" He looked at his sons again, in the same way that he had when Henry offered them supper. His shoulders rose and fell in a helpless shrug.

"You're right again, Mr. Walters; it is the only logical thing to do." He sighed and smiled wanly. "Logic is sometimes a difficult saddle to wear," he said gently. "But if one is a horse..."

It was a strange proverb, Henry thought. He wondered if Piper had just thought of it, or whether there actually was such a saying. "You're welcome to stay," he said redundantly.

"I know we are, Mr. Walters," Piper said with the same gentleness.

He stopped, and suddenly looked deep into Henry's eyes. "You are a very *rare* kind of man."

Again, Henry did not know what to say. Piper was smiling at him, but he could not even smile in return.

"I'll find some quilts for you. It's still cold, at night," he said. He felt the heat seep into his face at the gratuitousness of that last sentence, and left the kitchen hastily. He went up the stairs to the bedding closet, his face still warm. There were so many things to be careful of, in dealing with the Pipers; the most casual statements precipitated him into new traps of thoughtless offense.

He remembered what Piper had said about being over-careful of other people's sensibilities. The older man had been right, of course—for, among strangers, a man's toes were unwittingly trod on as often as he himself was liable to injure another. But the Pipers had themselves been painfully diffident.

Once again, one part of him wished that the Pipers had never come, and that, once here, they would be tracelessly gone in the morning. That part of him tried to persuade itself that the tactful Pipers would do exactly that.

But, already, another part of him was preparing itself for the following day, when he would have to stand on the hill and watch them back the car around in the cramped yard and roll down the hill—back the way they had come today, and the way they had gone that first, cold time, years ago.

THE NIGHT below the porch was full of bullfrog-song from the pond, which glinted faintly under the starlight. The night wind cut through the shrubs around the porch, and added its whisper.

Henry sat quietly in his chair, his field jacket shutting out the cold, a dead pipe in his teeth. His mind was blank— carefully blank. He had sat on this porch many nights in the past year, listening and learning, as the wind swept over the hills and the bullfrogs sang. At one time of the year, the wind was steady-blowing against the rain that waited over the mountains. At another time, the rain surged over the barrier; and then Henry listened to the sound of the brook that fed the pond, discovering how the water drained, what gullies it wore in the soil. He had lost part of a crop last year, because he did not know what the rain would do. He had learned, and this year there would be no loss.

He did not know where he had been given the patience to sit so, and learn. His father had had it, and he suspected that his grandfather had passed it on. That patience made him a farmer, for Nature could be understood; but she took a full four seasons to the year, and a man had to gear himself to the pace.

The Pipers had been good farmers, too. He had seen the signs, even through the blur that five years had dragged across their work. He knew as he sat there, that Harold Piper had spent his hours on this porch; listening, learning, planning—and dreaming.

He was hardly surprised when he heard the porch door open, and Piper coughed apologetically. "Mr. Walters?"

The night had given him calmness. "Come on out, Mr. Piper; you're welcome to a seat." But he was not sure of how stable his calm would have been if he were able to see the other man.

He heard him settle his weight into another chair. "Thank you." Then there was silence again, though several times Henry heard the sharp inhalation that a man makes when he starts to speak and changes his mind.

Finally, Piper said, "Mr. Walters, I'd like to tell you

something."

Henry frowned in the darkness, once again straining all his perceptions in an attempt to interpret the nuances of Piper's voice. There had been urgency, and fear of rebuff, and something else, as well. He could not penetrate that other, peculiar, quality. "Be glad to listen, Mr. Piper," he said.

Piper was quiet again for a moment, as though almost changing his mind. But then he sighed, and began. "I hope you'll understand. I think you will."

He paused, and Henry heard him chuckle for the first time—a low, resigned sound, that was a signal of surrender and relief at the struggle's end. "I—my sons and I—are not what we seem. Very few people are, of course, but, with us, the subterfuge is deeper."

Henry kept his eyes on the dimly seen pond, and listened patiently while Piper hunted out his words.

"I told you we left, when the war began. We did; we went back to my father's birthplace. I was born here, on this farm, as my sons were—" Henry winced. "—but my father came here when he was a young man. 'Piper' is not our real family name; it is a direct translation our name from my father's language."

"Germany?" Henry asked. "My grandparents came from Dessau. On the Elbe."

"No, Mr. Walters, I'm sorry." He paused again, and then said something in a language whose consonants leaped from crest to crest on the broad undercurrent of its vowels. There was a constrained quality to his voice, and he stopped in a moment. "I'm afraid my American accent's very thick. They had trouble understanding me, when we went back. My sons don't speak it at all, except for what they've picked up. It's a hard language to learn, unless you're born to it.

"Mr. Walters," he said suddenly, "when we went back, we had to go in a spaceship."

THE SENTENCE hung in the night air, and Henry found that he had raised his head involuntarily, and was looking up at the stars. 1966, A. D. Up there, somewhere, two gutted space-stations still swung. The American one, they said, was slowly losing speed, spiraling infinitesimally closer to the mother world, ready to break the web that held it to the sky. Someday, unless they got a rocket up and dismantled her, she'd spin into the ground and kill for the last time. But those stations were as far as man had gone.

One trembling step into the edge of the surf. "Go on, Mr. Piper," Henry said. *Speak, seafarer.*

"You see," Piper went on as though unaware that his audience might not believe him anymore, "the people on my father's world knew that war was coming. Technically, we weren't citizens of theirs any longer, but we all had relatives back on my father's world, and I suppose there was a lot of moral pressure on them. They sent ships to take us back, covering this whole planet, and picking up as many of us as possible in the time they had."

"Nobody saw them, huh?" Henry said.

"No, Mr. Walters, nobody really did. It wasn't easy, but a spaceship's lifeboats can be camouflaged to look like aircraft without much trouble. After that, of course, there is the difficulty of evading the strict checking systems, which are kept on scheduled flights; and some nations do not keep their skies as full of planes as others. But it was done, and most of us went. In some countries, only a few got by the travel restrictions that blocked their way to the rendezvous. Others didn't want to leave their homes; of course, there must have been a number who had forgotten where the old, long-unused landing places were, or who didn't care. After all, the greatest percentage of us were second generation citizens of our countries, and most of us had children."

Henry's breath caught in his throat for an instant. "Excuse me, Mr. Piper. That doesn't sound much like you people were any too well organized."

"What's your nationality, Mr. Walters?" Piper asked quietly.

"American. Uh—I see what you mean. I'm no more a German than you're a— It isn't Mars or Venus, is it?"

"No, Mr. Walters, it isn't; and I'm an American." The point was important to him, and he stressed it. "By birth. Racially, my people come from a world around a star pretty much like this one, not too far away." The embarrassment returned to his voice. "I'm sorry, but I don't think I'd better say which one." His voice grew sad, now.

"That world is older than yours, Mr. Walters, and it was never so fortunate in its natural riches. By my father's time, it was too late for conservation, for birth control, or hydroponics. It is always too late, for any world. One cannot be a miser, Mr. Walters, and still find time to push a civilization a little farther upward; a world cannot turn its energies inward, it cannot blunt the fine edge of its peoples' drive.

"A world is a spore pod. At first it is green, swelling with life. Then it dries up—but the pod bursts, and the spores go drifting out, and find fresh soil in which to grow."

The bullfrogs sang loudly in the pond, and the wind whispered over the hills.

"For my father, there was only poverty at home. They had the ships, and with them they found a few worlds. Some were unpopulated. Most of those were useless, for, if they had not developed life of their own; there was some ecological factor, which kept them from supporting transplanted life. Some, it is true, were suitable."

Piper stopped, and Henry turned to see his head silhouetted against the starlight. He, too, was looking up.

"It makes you wonder," Henry said. "If each world is like a spore pod... You don't look any different from an Earthman..."

"Yes," Piper said, "it does make you wonder, doesn't it?"

HENRY FILLED his pipe deliberately. He found a match in his pocket and puffed the tobacco alight, and while he did there was silence on the porch except for the soft sucking sound.

How far do you go? If you have engines, you must make automobiles. If you can roll at twenty miles per hour, you can fly at thirty. If you can, in one generation, transform thirty mph into five hundred and thirty; and that into sixteen hundred before the second generation is fairly begun; and that into seven miles per second, then you have left the Earth behind. And if your ships can touch a sister world two-hundred-forty-thousand miles away, no matter how arid that satellite—if you can do that today, then tomorrow you can go where the worlds are green, and at that rate...

How long before the spreading ships, thrusting through Andromeda, meet the ones that started in the opposite direction?

And Henry wondered, as he sat on the porch. But what he wondered was this: What was the speed of belief, as distinct from the velocity and acceleration of information?

"Go on, Mr. Piper," he said. He did not know.

"Their ships found other worlds, as well. Worlds already populated, but not yet overburdened. This world we're on now is the planet to which my father came.

"There were not many of his people who came to Earth. Of those, each individual was free to choose whatever way of life appealed to him the most. Different things attract different people. There were some in every country, before the war. My father brought his wife with him; together, they found work, learned the language and customs, and saved enough money to buy this farm."

Again, Henry shrank from something within himself.

"That was all he and my mother wanted, Mr. Walters. They died content; the farm was their fortune. I had married a girl—one of our own people, that I found in western New York State—and my parents left us the farm."

The frogs were beginning to quiet down a little. Henry felt the pressure of the wind against his cheek as it changed direction slightly, and frowned as he automatically noted its fitful rise and wane. It might rain by morning.

Piper sighed. "We had our sons; we worked the land." He stopped, and his voice changed quality. "I fought in the Second World War, Mr. Walters. Two and a half years in the Army." He chuckled again. "I was a corporal in the infantry."

Henry grunted. "You'd have to fight, wouldn't you? Can't get away from the government—though I'll bet you volunteered."

"I did, as a matter of fact." There was a short, self-conscious laugh. "I learned better than to do that again."

"Amen," said Henry with an identical laugh. And now that they had both gone through the conventional, lying, disclaimer, Henry had learned a little more about the pace with which belief overtakes information. He twisted in his chair and leaned toward Piper, trying to see him more clearly in the darkness. Damn it all, here he sat on a porch with a man whose ancestors had sprung up under another sun—a man who'd been in a spaceship!

HENRY FOUND himself grappling with a swelling impatience to prod the man on with his story. But he had no right to do that, and knew it. If Piper were to stop now, he could never have the right to question him, but would have to be content with what he already knew; for what Piper had seen and done and had happen in his life was Piper's personal store of memory—it was all the man had left, except for his sons.

"And then," Piper said as if he had felt Henry's urgency, "this war began to stir into life. This time, we had to leave. We could have stayed and fought as we'd fought before— fought each other, in a way; the same way you fought East Germans, Henry—but it wasn't the same kind of war anymore. This time, the civilians were really going to be hit. So the people from the mother planet came and evacuated us."

He sighed, the breath whispering between his teeth, and it took Henry a little while to realize that it meant he was biting his lower lip.

"I don't know," Piper said heavily. "I don't know if I would have stayed anyway, if I'd been alone. But Elizabeth wanted us to go; she had a lot of reasons, most of them good. I think she wanted it most because it meant the boys wouldn't have to go into one of the Services.

"I don't know whether that made us all cowards or not. We had responsibilities toward our country, and we ran out on them, that's sure. But every refugee from any war zone could be accused of the same thing. No civilian can really be expected to stay in a situation where he's going to be killed— particularly since he's not trained to fight back. Besides, how do you fight a cobalt bomb that goes off in the next state? Most civilians *had* to stick it—they didn't have any place to go; we did. Evacuate as many others as we could? Who's to pick and choose, and how much time did we have to convince anyone that we weren't going to eat them?

"Hell, we couldn't even step in and stop the war—not with any hope of not having this entire planet's population on our necks, howling for blood, as soon as they could develop starships of their own!

"The only thing I really regret is turning the boys into draft-dodgers against their will." His voice grew quietly proud. "They would have stayed, Henry... You know, they were all on the football team at Waterbury High? Made All-State with that team.

"But, you know how it is. The folks were pulling out on them—and, besides, any kid that age would give his left eye and right arm to ride a starship, and see another world."

"Wouldn't have to be a kid," Henry said with quiet hunger.

"No, no, I suppose not," Piper said. "Anyway—" He stopped, searching for words. When he found them, the faintly lyrical quality had returned to his sentences.

TWO GENERATIONS weren't enough, Henry thought—particularly not since he'd been back to the world his father came from. Enough to sever all the ties, certainly, but not to blot out the traditions and the history he'd learned from his father when he was a boy. Only people steeped in the Anglo-Saxon tradition of overt unsentimentality could speak of the lands of their fathers in light voices—and there was a reverence behind their flippancy when they did.

"We came back to my father's world. I can't tell you how many of us there were, in all, because I don't know. But it took three ships to take us.

"The world's name is Erelia—Erelia of the ice-blue seas. As with all planets, the word itself means simply, "the Earth," or "the world." It is the home—the one place in all the universe. And we, of course, were Erelians— "Earthmen."

He laughed, bitterly. The naked, unequivocal emotion of the sound raised the hackles of Henry's neck. Piper had never let down his guard so suddenly, or so completely.

"Poetry at midnight," Piper said in the voice of a man

mocking himself. "Listen to this:

> *One star beyond the brightest constellations burns,*
> *Hung at the raveled edge of the galactic rim,*
> *To which the farthest-traveled Earthman ever turns—*
> *Which through the distance and the dimness calls to him."*

"Pretty good," Henry said. He sat and thought about it for a moment. "One of your people write it?"

"Doggerel," Piper said shortly. "I wrote it."

Once again, there was that bitter laugh that struck across the face of the night. "The point is *where* I wrote it—and I wrote it on Erelia." His voice dropped, and re-assumed its mantle of gentle sadness. "You see, I wrote it about myself, and Earth—*this* Earth.

"Do you know what Erelia is—Erelia of the ice-blue seas?" he demanded with sudden fierceness and the phrase which had been loving, was now a brassy and sarcastic thing on his tongue. "It's a dust-bowl—a teeming, destitute dust-bowl! The seas *are* blue with ice, and the people huddle miserably around animal-chip fires in tottering huts. Poverty! My father spoke of poverty—poverty he fled from—and *he* loved that world.

"We came down on it—on a gravel plain that stretched as far as any of us could see. They had set up temporary housing for us—temporary, thin-skinned wooden housing that lasted us for five Earth years; eight of the bitter Winters. There wasn't another acre of land on that entire planet where they had room for us. They fed us on charity; they gave us food as good as they themselves ate, and some of us sickened and died on it. We lost five percent to pneumonia the first Winter.

"There's nothing left on that planet, Henry. The ships are based farther in—on the green worlds closer to the galactic center. The planet lives on sufferance—on whatever the colonized worlds can spare. There isn't a tool or a stick of wood or a scrap of cloth that hasn't got a fantastic value, and isn't carefully enumerated in the owner's last will and testament to be passed down to his heirs until it's worn to dust.

"They couldn't take us to one of the colonized worlds, because it would have been too far; it would have put too much of a drain on the economy when it was time to ship us back.

"And how they wanted to ship us back! They longed and ached and prayed for the day the war ended, and they could hurry us here—for we were breaking their backs. We—three shiploads to begin with, and dying like flies—were more than they could support. They took us in because they had to, and because they felt an obligation to us, I suppose. They gave us as good as they had—and it bled them white while we starved on it.

"The war ended, and they brought us back. They brought back what was left of us. Two shiploads—none too crowded. We turned pale, all of us, when we saw what had happened to the face of this planet. But they could not turn around to bring us back to Erelia. Again, it would have cost too much; and we would have killed Erelia for good and all. So, they left us. Those of us, who can somehow shoehorn ourselves back into this society, will. Those who cannot will be picked up, if there are enough of them to be worth it, and will be taken somewhere else. To a colonized world if we're lucky—if they find one whose ecology can take us. If not, to another world such as this, to begin the assimilation process all over again."

HENRY HAD sat, listening as though weathering a storm. His face worked itself into a mask of the deepest pity he had ever known—and now he was terribly glad of the darkness.

"That bad, Harold?" he asked gently. "Is it? Was it? I know you lost your wife, and it's hard, but they were doing the best they could."

"I know." The resigned words fell quietly, muffled, as though Piper held his face in his hands. Then his voice cleared, but clung to its resignation. "Everyone does the best he can; the Erelians are doing theirs. It's only on Erelia itself that things are so bad, and that will be over in another generation or two. They will spread out, and their people will begin to live again.

"But, meanwhile, there are...backwashes. Like my sons and myself."

He stood up suddenly, pushing his chair back. "Henry, I've trusted you with something that only one or two other native Earthmen know. My sons and I will leave in the morning, and you will never see us again. I don't suppose it matters, really, whether you try to pass on what I've told you to anyone else. Some of them won't believe you, and others will say they don't. Do what you think best." His voice became brooding. "I've seen Earth from space, Henry. It won't be long before the rockets go out, searching; they'll find Erelia soon enough."

He opened the porch door and stood half inside the house. "It's very late, Henry; all of us need sleep. Good night." The door closed behind him.

Henry let him go. Piper had talked himself out—had laid his emotions bare before a man he hadn't known for twelve hours.

And so Henry sat, for many more hours, thinking, while the stars wheeled by overhead and the misty wind edged over the mountains and obscured them.

IT WAS RAINING when Henry and the Pipers ate breakfast as silently as they had eaten supper, and the droplets rebounded from the roof of the car as Henry stood on the back porch and watched Piper start the motor. He had shaken hands with all four of them, and accepted their diffident thanks once more. He had started to speak a number of times, but stopped each time. Piper had not referred to what had been said on the porch; this morning his face was as Henry remembered it from yesterday, and not at all like the one that Henry had pictured beside him in the darkness.

But now the barrier broke in his throat, and just as Piper began to crank up his window, he shouted, "Wait!"

Something flickered over Piper's face—a sad smile, and, somehow, a knowing one. "Wait for me a minute," he told his sons, and came out of the car, dashing across the narrow strip of yard to the shelter of the porch.

"Harold—" Henry began.

"No, Henry," Piper said, cutting him off. The sad, wise smile touched his face again. "No, we can't stay; we don't belong any more. This is your land—your world. It may be my world, too, but the claim's less certain. This Earth is your heritage, and I could not rob you. My heritage is wandering, in search of a home. Not a borrowed one, but one we can make our own. I owe it to my sons, Henry," he said quietly. "We'll try further north. There might be some land there. If not—" He shrugged and turned his eyes on the car, once more looking at his sons. "If not, then we will go to another world. And if not that one," he admitted, "then somewhere else. It would be unjust to take from another, and steal a birthright." He reached out and shook Henry's hand for the last time. "Goodbye, Henry."

"Goodbye, Harold... Good luck."

HE STOOD on the hillside, disregarding the rain, and saw the car bump down the narrow road, toward the highway that ran north. He did not know. He looked around at the land, soaking under the rain, and was not sure.

A backwash, Piper had called himself and his sons. And, perhaps he was right. Perhaps it was true that his race's real future was on the planets that were found new, and young, and undeveloped. In the light of historical logic, the Pipers were misplaced, a casual offshoot—doomed to wither—of the sudden outward burst of their people. Then, it was true that they had no right to add themselves as a burden to this planet; and it would have been unjust to take what he had been ready to offer, finally.

But with only a few worlds capable of being colonized... And all of Erelia's billions, surging to be free of their wan planet...

Justice was a blind goddess, holding a two-edged sword, and Henry wondered if she did not sometimes scar herself.

Only a few worlds. He thought of the Pipers, searching for land to buy when there was no land, except for what the government held in reserve for the men who had finally managed to save some of it. And while he stood, and watched the car go over the last rise in the road, the rain fell and fed the brook with muddy water.

THE END

Seven Came Back

By
CLIFFORD D. SIMAK

*It was easy for Adam and Eve; but on Mars it took seven to
maintain the birth rate!*

THEY CAME out of the Martian night, six pitiful little
creatures looking for a seventh. They stopped at the edge of the
campfire's lighted circle and stood there, staring at the three
Earthmen with their owlish eyes.

The Earthmen froze at whatever they were doing.

"Quiet," said Wampus Smith, talking out of the corner of his
bearded lips. "They'll come in if we don't make a move."

From far away came a faint, low moaning, floating in across
the wilderness of sand and jagged pinnacles of rock and the
great stone buttes.

The six stood just at the firelight's edge. The reflection of
the flames touched their fur with highlights of red and blue and
their bodies seemed to shimmer against the backdrop of the
darkness on the desert.

"Venerables," Nelson said to Richard Webb across the fire.

Webb's breath caught in his throat. Here was a thing he had
never hoped to see. A thing that no human being could ever
hope to see.

Six of the Venerables of Mars walking in out of the desert
and the darkness, standing in the firelight. There were many
men, he knew, who would claim that the race was now extinct,
hunted down, trapped out, hounded to extinction by the greed
of the human sand men.

The six had seemed the same at first, six beings without a
difference; but now, as Webb looked at them, he saw those
minor points of bodily variation which marked each one of

them as a separate individual. Six of them, Webb thought, and there should be seven.

Slowly they came forward, walking deeper into the campfire's circle. One by one they sat down on the sand facing the three men. No one said a word and the tension built up in the circle of the fire while far toward the north the thing kept up its keening, like a sharp, thin knife blade cutting through the night.

"Human glad," Wampus Smith said finally, talking in the patois of the desert. "He waited long."

One of the creatures spoke, its words half English, half Martian, all of it pure gibberish to the ear that did not know.

"We die," it said. "Human hurt for long. Human help some now. Now we die, human help?"

"Human sad," said Wampus and even while he tried to make his voice sad, there was elation in it, a trembling eagerness, a quivering as a hound will quiver when the scent is hot.

"We are six," the creature said. "Six not enough. We need another one. We do not find the seven, we die. Race die forever now."

"Not forever," Smith told them.

THE VENERABLE insisted on it.
"Forever. They're other sixes. No other seven."
"How can human help?"
"Human know. Human have Seven somewhere?"
Wampus shook his head.
"Where we have Seven?"
"In cage. On Earth. For human to see."
Wampus shook his head again.
"No Seven on Earth."
"There was one," Webb said softly. "In a zoo."
"Zoo," said the creature, tonguing the unfamiliar word. "We mean that. In cage."
"It died," said Webb. "Many years ago."
"Human have one," the creature insisted. "Here on planet. Hid out. To trade."

"No understand," said Wampus but Webb knew from the way he said it that he understood.

"Find Seven. Do not kill it. Hide it. Knowing we come. Knowing we pay."

"Pay? What pay?"

"City," said the creature. "Old city."

"That's your city," Nelson said to Webb. "The ruins you are hunting."

"Too bad we haven't got a Seven," Wampus said. "We could hand it over, and they'd lead us to the ruins."

"Human hurt for long," the creature said. "Human kill all Sevens. Have good fur. Women human wear it. High pay for Seven fur."

"Lord, yes," said Nelson. "Fifty thousand for one at the trading post. A cool half million for a four-skin cape made up in New York."

Webb sickened at the thought of it, at the casual way in which Nelson mentioned it. It was illegal now, of course, but the law had come too late to save the Venerables. Although a law, come to think of it, should not have been necessary. A human being, in all rightness...an intelligent form of life, in all rightness, should not hunt down and kill another intelligent being to strip off its pelt and sell it for fifty thousand dollars.

"No Seven hid," Wampus was saying. "Law says friends. No dare hurt Seven. No dare hide Seven."

"Law far off," said the creature. "Human his own law."

"Not us," said Wampus. "We don't monkey with the law."

And that's a laugh, thought Webb.

"You help?" asked the creature.

"Try, maybe," Wampus told them cagily. "No good, though. You can't find. Human can't find."

"You find. We show city."

"We watch," said Wampus. "Close watch. See Seven, bring it. Where you be?"

"Canyon mouth."

"Good," said Wampus. "Deal?"

"Deal," said the creature.

Slowly the six of them got to their feet and turned back to the night again.

At the edge of the fire-lit circle they stopped. The spokesman turned back to the three men.

"By," he said.

"Good-by," said Wampus.

Then they were gone, back into the desert.

THE THREE men sat and listened for a long time, not knowing what they listened for, but with ears taut to hear the slightest sound, trying to read out of sound some of the movement of life that surged all around the fire.

On Mars, thought Webb, one always listens. That is the survival price. To watch and listen and be still and quiet. And ruthless, too. To strike before another thing can strike. To see or hear a danger and be ready for it, be half a second quicker than it is quick. And to recognize that cycle once you see or hear it.

Finally Nelson took up again the thing he had been doing when the six arrived, whetting his belt knife to razor sharpness on a pocket whetstone.

The soft, sleek whirr of metal traveling over stone sounded like a heartbeat, a pulse that did not originate within the firelight circle, but something that came out of the darkness, the pulse and beat of the wilderness itself.

Wampus said: "It's too bad, Lars, that we don't know where to pick us up a Seven."

"Yeah," said Lars.

"Might turn a good deal," Wampus said. "Likely to be treasure in that old city. All the stories say so."

Nelson grunted. "Just stories."

"Stones," said Wampus. "Stones so bright and polished they could put your eyes out. Sacks of them. Tire a man out just packing them away."

"Wouldn't need more than one load," Nelson declared. "Just

one load would set you up for life."

Webb saw that both of them were looking at him, squinting their eyes against the firelight.

He said, almost angrily: "I don't know about the treasure."

"You heard the stories," Wampus said.

Webb nodded. "Let's say it this way. I'm not interested in the treasure. I don't expect to find any."

"Wouldn't mind if you did, would you?" Lars asked.

"It doesn't matter," Webb told him. "One way or the other."

"What do you know about this city?" Wampus demanded and it wasn't just conversation, it was a question asked with an answer expected, for a special purpose. "You been muttering around and dropping hints here and there but you never came cold out and told us."

For a moment, Webb stared at the man. Then he spoke slowly. "Just this. I figured out where it might be. From a knowledge of geography and geology and some understanding of the rise of cultures. I figured where the grass and wood and water would have been when Mars was new and young. I tried to locate, theoretically, the likeliest place for a civilization to arise. That's all there's to it."

"And you never thought of treasure?"

"I thought of finding out something about the Martian culture," Webb said. "How it rose and why it fell and what it might be like."

Wampus spat. "You aren't even sure there is a city," he said disgustedly.

"Not until just now," said Webb. "Now I know there is."

"From what them little critters said?"

Webb nodded. "From what they said. That's right."

Wampus grunted and was silent.

Webb watched the two across the campfire from him.

They think I'm soft, he thought. They despise me because I'm soft. They would leave me in a minute if it served their purpose or they'd put a knife into me without a second thought if that should serve their purpose...if there was something that I had they wanted.

There had been no choice, he realized. He could not have gone alone into this wilderness, for if he'd tried he probably wouldn't have lived beyond the second day. It took special knowledge to live here and a special technique and a certain kind of mind. A man had to develop a high survival factor to walk into Mars beyond the settlements.

And the settlements now were very far away. Somewhere to the east.

"Tomorrow," Wampus said, "we change directions. We go north instead of west."

Webb said nothing. His hand slid around cautiously and touched the gun at his belt, to make sure that it was there.

IT HAD BEEN a mistake to hire these two, he knew. But probably none of the others would have been better. They were all of a breed, a toughened, vicious band of men who roamed the wilderness, hunting, trapping, mining, taking what they found. Wampus and Nelson had been the only two at the post when he had arrived. All the other sand men had gone a week before, back to their hunting grounds.

At first they had been respectful, almost fawning. But as the days went on they felt surer of their ground and had grown insolent. Now Webb knew that he'd been taken for a sucker. The two stayed at the post he knew now, for no other reason than that they were without a grubstake. He was that grubstake. He supplied them with the trappings they needed to get back into the wilderness. Once he had been a grubstake, now he was a burden.

"I said," declared Wampus, "that tomorrow we go north."

Webb still said nothing.

"You heard me, didn't you?" asked Wampus.

"The first time," Webb said.

"We go north," said Wampus, "and we travel fast."

"You got a Seven staked out somewhere?"

Lars snickered. "Ain't that the damnedest thing you ever

heard of? Takes seven of them. Now with us, it just takes a man and woman."

"I asked you," said Webb to Wampus, "if you have a Seven caged up somewhere?"

"No," said Wampus. "We just go north, that's all."

"I hired you to take me west."

Wampus snarled at him. "I thought you'd say that, Webb. I just wanted to know exactly how you felt about it."

"You want to leave me stranded here," said Webb. "You took my money and agreed to guide me. Now you have something else to do. You either have a Seven or you think you know where you can find one. And if I knew and talked, you would be in danger. So there's only one of two things that you can do with me. You can kill me or you can leave me and let something else do the job for you."

Lars said: "We're giving you a choice, ain't we?"

Webb looked at Wampus and, the man nodded. "You got your choice, Webb."

He could go for his gun, of course. He could get one of them, most likely, before the other one got him. But there would be nothing gained. He would be just as dead as if they shot him out of hand. As far as that went he was as good as dead anyhow, for hundreds of miles stretched between him and the settlements and even if he were able to cross those many miles there was no guarantee that he could find the settlements.

"We're moving out right now," said Wampus. "Ain't smart to travel in the dark, but ain't the first time that we had to do it. We'll be up north in a day or two."

Lars nodded. "Once we get back to the settlements, Webb, we'll h'ist a drink to you."

Wampus joined in the spirit of the moment. "Good likker, Webb. We can afford good likker then."

WEBB SAID nothing, did not move. He sat on the ground, relaxed.

And that, he told himself, was the thing that scared him.

That he could sit and know what was about to happen and be so unconcerned about it.

Perhaps it had been the miles of wilderness that made it possible, the harsh, raw land and the vicious life that moved across the land…the ever-hungering, ever-hunting life that prowled and stalked and killed. Here life was stripped to its essentials and one learned that the line between life and death was a thin line at best.

"Well," said Wampus finally, "what will it be, Webb."

"I think," said Webb, gravely, "I think I'll take my chance on living."

Lars clucked his tongue against his teeth. "Too bad," he said. "We was hoping it'd be the other way around. Then we could take all the stuff. As it is, we got to leave you some."

"You can always sneak back," said Webb, "and shoot me as I sit here. It would be an easy thing."

"That," said Wampus, "is not a bad idea."

Lars said: "Give me your gun, Webb. I'll throw it back to you when we leave. But we ain't taking a chance of you plugging us while we're getting ready."

Webb lifted his gun out of its holster and handed it over. Still sitting where he was, he watched them pack and stow the supplies into the wilderness wagon.

Finally it was done.

"We're leaving you plenty to last," Wampus told him. "More than enough."

"Probably," said Webb. "You figure I can't last very long."

"If it was me," said Wampus, "I'd take it quick and easy."

Webb sat for a long time, listening to the motor of the wagon until it was out of hearing, then waiting for the gun blast that would send him toppling face forward into the flaming campfire.

But finally he knew that it would not come. He piled more fuel on the fire and crawled into his sleeping bag.

IN THE morning he headed east, following backward along

the tracks of the wilderness wagon. They'd guide him, he knew, for a week or so, but finally they would disappear, brushed out by drifting sand and by the action of the weak and whining wind that sometimes blew across the bleakness of the wilderness.

Anyhow, while he followed them he would know at least that he was going in the right direction. Although more than likely he would be dead before they faded out, for the wilderness crawled with too much sudden death to be sure of living from one moment to the next.

He walked with the gun hanging in his hand, watching every side, stopping at the top of the ridges to study the terrain in front of him before he moved down into it.

The unaccustomed pack, which he had fashioned inexpertly out of his sleeping bag, grew heavier as the day progressed and chafed his shoulders raw. The sun was warm...as warm as the night would be cold...and thirst mounted in his throat to choke him. Carefully he doled out sips of water from the scanty supply the two had left him.

He knew he would not get back. Somewhere between where he stood and the settlements he would die of lack of water or of an insect bite or beneath the jaws and fangs of some charging beast or from sheer exhaustion.

There was, once you thought it out, no reason why a man should try to get back...since there was utterly no chance that he would get back. But Webb didn't stop to reason it out; he set his face toward the east and followed the wagon tracks.

For there was a *humanness* in him that said he must try at least...that he must go as far as he could go, that he must avoid death as long as he could. So on he went, going as far as he could go and avoiding death.

He spotted the ant colony in time to circle it, but he circled it too closely and the insects, catching scent of food within their grasp, streamed out after him. It took a mile of running before he outdistanced them.

He saw the crouching beast camouflaged against the sand, where it was waiting for him, and shot it where it lay. Later in the day, when another monstrosity came tearing out from behind a rock outcropping, his bullet caught it between the eyes before it had covered half the distance.

For an hour he squatted, unmoving, on the sand, while a huge insect that looked like a bumblebee, but wasn't, hunted for the thing that it had sighted only a moment before. But since it could recognize a thing through motion only, it finally gave up and went away. Webb stayed squatting for another half hour against the chance that it had not gone away, but was lurking somewhere watching for the motion it had sighted to take up again.

These times he avoided death, but he knew that the hour would come when he would not see a danger, or having seen it, would not move fast enough to stop it.

THE MIRAGES came to haunt him, to steal his eyes from the things that he should be watching. Mirages that flickered in the sky, with their feet upon the ground. Tantalizing pictures of things that could not be on Mars, of places that might have been at one time...but that very long ago.

Mirages of broad, slow rivers with the slant of sail upon them. Mirages of green forests that stretched across the hills and so clear, so close that one could see the little clumps of wild flowers that grew among the trees. And in some of them the hint of snowcapped mountains, in a world that knew no mountains.

He kept a watch for fuel as he went along, hoping to find a cache of "embalmed" wood cropping out of the sand...wood left over from that dim age when these hills and valleys had been forest covered, wood that had escaped the ravages of time and now lay like the dried mummies of trees in the aridness of the desert.

But there was none to be found and he knew that more than likely he would have to spend a fireless night. He could not spend a night in the open without fire. If he tried it, he would be gobbled up an hour after twilight had set in.

He must somehow find shelter in one of the many caves of the weird rock formations that sprang out of the desert. Find a cave and clean out whatever might be in it, block its entrance with stones and boulders and sleep with gun in hand.

It had sounded easy when he thought of it, but while there were many caves, he was forced to reject them one by one since each of them had too large an opening to be closed against attack. A cave, he knew, with an unclosed mouth, would be no better than a trap.

The sun was less than an hour high when he finally spotted a cave that would serve the purpose, located on a ledge of stone jutting out of a steep hill.

From the bottom he stood long minutes surveying the hill. Nothing moved. There was no telltale fleck of color.

Slowly, he started up, digging his feet into the shifting talus of the slope, fighting his way up foot by foot, stopping for long minutes to regain his breath and to survey the slope ahead.

Gaining the ledge, he moved cautiously toward the cave, gun leveled, for there was no telling what might come out of it.

He debated on his next move.

Flash his light inside to see what was there?

Or simply thrust his gun into the opening and spray the inside with its lethal charge?

There could be no squeamishness, he told himself. Better to kill a harmless thing than to run the chance of passing up a danger.

He heard no sound until the claws of the thing were scrabbling on the ledge behind him. He shot one quick glance over his shoulder and saw the beast almost on top of him, got the impression of gaping mouth and murderous fangs and tiny eyes that glinted with a stony cruelty.

There was no time to turn and fire. There was time for just one thing.

HIS LEGS moved like driving pistons, hurling his body at the cave. The stone lip of it caught his shoulder and ripped through his clothing, gashing his arm, but he was through, through and rolling free. Something brushed his face and he rolled over something that protested in a squeaking voice and off in one corner there was a thing that mewed quietly to itself.

On his knees, Webb swung his gun around to face the opening of the cave, saw the great bulk of the beast that had charged him trying to squeeze its way inside.

It backed away and then a great paw came in, feeling this way and that, hunting for the food that crouched inside the cave.

Mouths jabbered at Webb, a dozen voices speaking in the lingo of the desert and he heard them say: "Human, human, kill, kill, kill."

Webb's gun spat and the paw went limp and was pulled slowly from the cave. The great grey body toppled and they heard it strike the slope below the ledge and go slithering away down the talus slope.

"Thanks, human," said the voices. "Thanks, human."

Slowly Webb sat down, cradling the gun in his lap.

All around him he heard the stir of life.

Sweat broke out on his forehead and he felt moisture running from his armpits down his sides.

What was in the cave? What was in here with him?

That they had talked to him didn't mean a thing. Half the so-called animals of Mars could talk the desert lingo, a vocabulary of a few hundred words, part of them Earthian, part of them Martian, part of them God-knew-what.

For here on Mars many of the animals were not animals at all, but simply degenerating forms of life that at one time, must have formed a complex civilization. The Venerables, who still retained some of the shape of bipeds, would have reached the highest culture, but there must have been many varying degrees of culture, living by compromise or by tolerance.

"Safe," a voice told him. "Trust. Cave law."

"Cave law?"

"Kill in cave…no. Kill outside cave…yes. Safe in cave."

"I no kill," said Webb. "Cave law good."

"Human know cave law?"

Webb said: "Human keep cave law."

"Good," the voice told him. "All safe now."

Webb relaxed. He slipped his gun into his holster and took off his pack, laid it down alongside and rubbed his raw and blistered shoulders.

He could believe these things, he told himself. A thing so elemental and so simple as cave law was a thing that could be understood and trusted. It arose from a basic need, the need of the weaker life forms to forget their mutual differences and their mutual preying upon one another at the fall of night...the need to find a common sanctuary against the bigger and the more vicious and the lonely killers who took over with the going of the sun.

A voice said. "Come light. Human kill."

Another voice said: "Human keep cave law in dark. No cave law in light. Human kill come light."

"Human no kill come light," said Webb.

"All human kill," said one of the things. "Human kill for fur. Human kill for food. We fur. We food."

"This human never kill," said Webb. "This human friend."

"Friend?" one of them, asked. "We not know friend. Explain friend."

Webb didn't try. There was no use, he knew. They could not understand the word. It was foreign to this wilderness.

At last he asked: "Rocks here?"

One of the voices answered:

"Rocks in cave. Human want rocks?"

"Pile in cave mouth," said Webb. "No killer get in."

They digested that for awhile. Finally one of them spoke up: "Rock good."

They brought rocks and stones and, with Webb helping them, wedged the cave mouth tight.

IT WAS TOO dark to see the things, but they brushed against him as they worked and some of them were soft and furry and others had hides like crocodiles, that tore his skin as he brushed against them. And there was one that was soft and pulpy and gave him the creeps.

He settled down in one corner of the cave with his sleeping bag between his body and the wall. He would have liked to crawl into it, but that would have meant unpacking and if he unpacked his supplies, he knew there'd be none come morning.

Perhaps, he reasoned, the body heat of all the things in here will keep the cave from getting too cold. Cold, yes, but not too cold for human life. It was, he knew, a gamble at best.

Sleep at night in friendship, kill one another and flee from one another with the coming of the dawn. Law, they called it. Cave law. Here was one for the books; here was something that was not even hinted at in all the archaeological tomes that he had ever read.

And he had read them all. There was something here on Mars that fascinated him. A mystery and a loneliness, an emptiness and a retrogression that haunted him and finally sent him out to try to pierce some of that mystery, to try to hunt for the reason for that retrogression, to essay, to measure the greatness of the culture that in some far dim period had come tumbling down.

There has been some great work done along that line. Axelson with his scholarly investigation of the symbolic water jugs and Mason's sometimes fumbling attempt to trace the great migrations. Then there was Smith, who had traveled the barren world for years jotting down the windblown stories whispered by the little degenerating things about an ancient greatness and a golden past. Myths, most of them, of course, but some place, somewhere lay the answer to the origin of the myths. Folklore does not leap full-blown from the mind; it starts with a fact and that fact is added to and the two facts are distorted and you have a myth. But at the bottom, back of all of it, is the starting point of fact.

So it was, so it must be with the myth that told about the great and glowing city that had stood above all other things of

Mars…a city that was known to the far ends of the planet.

A place of culture, Webb told himself, a place where all the achievements and all the dreams and every aspiration of the once-great planet would have come together.

And yet, in more than a hundred years of hunting and of digging, Earth's archaeologists had found no trace of any city, let alone that city of all cities. Kitchen middens and burial places and wretched huddling places where broken remnants of the great people had lived for a time…there were plenty of these. But no great city.

It must be somewhere, Webb was convinced. That myth could not lie, for it was told too often at too many different places by too many different animals that had once been people.

Mars fascinated me, he thought, and it still fascinates me, but now it will be the death of me…for there's death in its fascination. Death in the lonely stretches and death waiting on the buttes. Death in this cave, too, for they may kill me come the morning to prevent me killing them; they may keep their truce of the night just long enough to make an end of me.

The law of the cave? Some holdover from the ancient day, some memory of a now forgotten brotherhood? Or a device necessitated by the evil days that had come when the brotherhood had broken?

HE LAID his head back against the rock and closed his eyes and thought…if they kill me, they kill me, but I will not kill them. For there has been too much human killing on the planet Mars. I will repay part of the debt at least. I will not kill the ones who took me in.

He remembered himself creeping along the ledge outside the cave, debating whether he should have a look first or stick in the muzzle of his gun and sweep the cave as a simple way of being sure there would be nothing there to harm him.

"I did not know," he said. "I did not know."

A soft furry body brushed against him and a voice spoke to him.

"Friend means no hurt? Friend means no kill?"

"No hurt," said Webb. "No kill."

"You saw six?" the voice asked.

Webb jerked from the wall and sat very still.

"You saw six?" the voice was insistent.

"I saw six," said Webb.

"When?"

"One sun."

"Where six?"

"Canyon mouth," said Webb. "Wait at canyon mouth."

"You hunt Seven?"

"No," said Webb. "I go home."

"Other humans?"

"They north," said Webb. "They hunt Seven north."

"They kill Seven?"

"Catch seven," said Webb. "Take Seven to six. See city."

"Six promise?"

"Six promise," said Webb.

"You good human. You friend human. You no kill Seven."

"No kill" insisted Webb.

"All humans kill. Kill Seven sure. Seven good fur. Much pay. Many Sevens die for human."

"Law says no kill," declared Webb. "Human law says Seven friend. No kill friend."

"Law? Like cave law?"

"Like cave law," said Webb.

"You good friend of Seven?"

"Good friend of all," said Webb.

"I Seven," said the voice.

Webb sat quietly and let the numbness clear out of his brain.

"Seven," he finally said. "You go canyon mouth. Find six. They wait. Human friend glad."

"Human friend want city," said the creature. "Seven friend to human. Human find Seven. Human see city. Six promise."

Webb almost laughed aloud in bitterness. Here, at last, the chance that he had hoped might come. Here, at last, the thing that he had wanted, the thing he had come to Mars to do. And he couldn't do it. He simply couldn't do it.

"Human no go," he said. "Human die. No food. No water. Human die."

"We care for human," Seven told him. "No friend human before. All kill humans. Friend human come. We care for it."

Webb was silent for a while, thinking.

Then he asked: "You give human food? You find human water?"

"Take care," said Seven.

"How Seven know I saw six?"

"Human tell. Human think. Seven know."

So that was it…telepathy. Some vestige of a former power, some attribute of a magnificent culture, not quite forgotten yet. How many of the other creatures in this cave would have it, too?

"Human go with Seven?" Seven asked.

"Human go," said Webb.

He might as well, he told himself. Going east, back toward the settlements, was no solution to his problem. He knew he'd never reach the settlements. His food would run out. His water would run out. Some beast would catch him and make a meal of him. He didn't have a chance.

Going with the little creature that stood beside him in the darkness of the cave, he might have a chance. Not too good a chance, perhaps, but at least a chance. There would be food and water or at least a chance of food and water. There would be another helping him to watch for the sudden death that roamed the wilderness. Another one to warn him, to help him recognize the danger.

"Human cold," said Seven.

"Cold," admitted Webb.

"One cold," said Seven. "Two warm."

The furry thing crawled into his arms, put its arms around his body. After a moment, he put his arms around it.

"Sleep," said Seven. "Warm. Sleep."

WEBB ATE the last of his food and the Seven Venerables told him: "We care."

"Human die," Webb insisted. "No food. Human die."

"We take care," the seven little creatures told him, standing in a row. "Later we take care."

So he took it to mean that there was no food for him now, but later there would be.

They took up the march again.

It was an interminable thing, that march. A thing to make a man cry out in his sleep. A thing to shiver over when they had been lucky enough to find wood and sat hunched around the fire. Day after endless day of sand and rock, of crawling up to a high ridge and plunging down the other side, of slogging through the heat across the level land that had been sea bottom in the days long gone.

It became a song, a drum beat, a three-note marching cadence that rang through the human's head, an endless thing that hammered in his brain through the day and stayed with him hours after they had stopped for night. Until he was dizzy with it, until his brain was drugged with the hammer of it, so that his eyes refused to focus and the gun bead was a fuzzy globe when he had to use the weapon against the crawling things and charging things and flying things that came at them out of nowhere.

Always there were the mirages, the everlasting mirages of Mars that seemed to lie just beneath the surface of reality. Flickering pictures painted in the sky the water and the trees and the long green sweep of grass that Mars had not known for countless centuries. As if, Webb told himself, the past were very close behind them, as if the past might still exist and was trying to catch up, reluctant to be left behind in the march of time.

He lost count of the days and steeled himself against the speculation of how much longer it might be, until it seemed that it would go on forever, that they would never stop, that they would face each morning the barren wilderness they must stagger through until the fall of night.

He drank the last of the water and reminded them he could not live without it.

"Later," they told him. "Water later."

THAT WAS the day they came to the city and there, deep in a tunnel far beneath the topmost ruins there was water, water dripping, drop by slow and tantalizing drop from a broken pipe. Dripping water and that was a wondrous thing on Mars.

The seven drank sparingly since they had been steeled for century upon century to get along with little water, until they had adapted themselves to get along with little water and it was no hardship for them. But Webb lay for hours beside the broken pipe, holding cupped hands for a little to collect before he lapped it down, lying there in the coolness that was a blessed thing.

He slept and awoke and drank again and he was rested and was no longer thirsty, but his body cried for food. And there was no food, and none to get him food. For the little ones were gone.

They will come back, he said. They are gone for just a little while and will be back again. They have gone to get me food and they will bring it to me. And he thought very kindly of them.

He picked his way upward through the tunnel down which they'd come and so at last came to the ruins that lay on the hill that thrust upward from the surrounding country so that when one stood on the hill's top, there was miles of distance, dropping away on every side.

There wasn't much that one could see of the ruined city. It would have been entirely possible to have walked past the hill and not have known the city was there. During thousands of years it had crumbled and fallen in upon itself and some of it had dissolved to dust and the sand had crept in and covered it and sifted among its fragments until it simply was a part of the hill.

Here and there Webb found broken fragments of chiseled masonry and here and there a shard of pottery, but a man could have walked past these, if he had not been looking, and taken them for no more than another rock scattered among the trillions of other fragmentary rocks littered on the surface of the planet.

The tunnel, he found, led down into the bowels of the fallen city, into the burial mound of the fallen greatness and the vanished glory of a proud people whose descendants now scuttled animal-like in the ancient deserts and talked in an idiom that was no more than a memory of the literacy that must have flourished once in the city on the hill.

In the tunnel Webb found evidence of solid blocks of carven stone, broken columns, paving blocks and something that seemed at one time to have been a beautifully executed statue.

At the end of the tunnel, he cupped his hands at the pipe and drank again, then went back to the surface and sat on the ground beside the tunnel mouth and stared out across the emptiness of Mars.

It would take power and tools and many men to uncover and sift the evidence of the city. It would take years of painstaking, scholarly work...and he didn't even have a shovel. And worst of all, he had no time. For if the seven did not show up with food he would one day go down into the darkness of the tunnel and there eventually join his human dust with the ancient dust of this alien world.

There had been a shovel, he remembered, and Wampus and Lars when they deserted him, had left it for him. A rare consideration, surely he told himself. But of the supplies, which he had carried away from the campfire, that long gone morning there were just two things left, his sleeping bag and the pistol at his belt. All else he could get along without, those two were things that he had to have.

An archaeologist, he thought. An archaeologist sitting on top of the greatest find that any archaeologist had ever made and not able to do a single thing about it.

Wampus and Lars had thought that there would be treasure here. And there was no certain treasure, no treasure revealed and waiting for the hands of men to take. He had thought of glory and there was no glory. He had thought of knowledge and without a shovel and some time there simply was no knowledge. No knowledge beyond the bare knowing that he had been right, that the city did exist.

And yet there was certain other knowledge gained along the way. The knowledge that the seven types of the Venerables did still in fact exist, that from this existence the race might still continue despite the guns and snares and the greed and guile of Earthmen who had hunted Seven for its fifty thousand dollar pelt.

Seven little creatures, seven different sexes. All of them essential to the continuance of the race. Six little creatures looking for the seventh and he had found the seventh. Because he had found the seventh, because he had been the messenger, there would be at least one new generation of the Venerables to carry on the race.

What use, he thought, to carry on a race that had failed its purpose?

He shook his head.

You can't play God, he said. You can't presume to judge. There either is a purpose in all things or there's no purpose in anything, and who is there to know?

There either is purpose that I reached this city or there is no purpose. There is a purpose that I may die here or it is possible that my dying here will be no more than another random factor in the great machination of pure chance that moves the planets through their courses and brings a man homeward at the end of day.

And there was another knowledge...the knowledge of the endless reaches and the savage loneliness that was the Martian wilderness. The knowledge of that and the queer, almost non-human detachment that it fused into the human soul.

Lessons, he thought.

The lesson that one man is an insignificant flyspeck crawling across the face of eternity. The lesson that one life is a relatively unimportant thing when it stands face to face with the over-riding reality of the miracle of all creation.

He got up and stood at his full height and knew his insignificance and his humility in the empty sweep of land that fell away on every side and in the arching sky that vaulted over-head from horizon to horizon and the utter silence that lay upon the land and sky.

STARVING was a lonely and an awful business.

Some deaths are swift and clean.

But starving is not one of these.

The seven did not come. Webb waited for them, and because he still felt kindly toward them, he found excuses for them. They did not realize, he told himself, how short a time a man may go without nourishment. The strange mating, he told himself, involving seven personalities, probably was a complicated procedure and might take a great deal more time than one usually associated with such phenomena. Or something might have happened to them, they might be having trouble of their own. As soon as they had worked it out, they would come, and they would bring him food.

So he starved with kindly thoughts and with a great deal more patience than a man under dissimilar circumstances might be expected to.

And he found, even when he felt the lassitude of under-nourishment creeping along his muscles and his bones, even when the sharp pangs of hunger had settled to a gnawing horror that never left him, even when he slept, that his mind was not affected by the ravages that his body was undergoing; that his brain, apparently, was sharpened by the lack of food, that it seemed to step aside from his tortured body and become a separate entity that drew in upon itself and knotted all its faculties into a hardbound bundle that was scarcely aware of external factors.

He sat for long hours upon a polished rock, perhaps part of that once proud city, which he found just a few yards from the tunnel mouth, and stared out across the sun-washed wilderness which stretched for miles toward a horizon that it never seemed to reach. He sought for purpose with a sharp-edged mind that probed at the roots of existence and of happenstance and sought to evolve out of the random factors that moved beneath the surface of the universe's orderliness some evidence of a pattern that would be understandable to the human mind. Often he thought he had it, but it always slid away from him like quicksilver escaping from a clutching hand.

If Man ever was to find the answer, he knew, it must be in a place like this, where there was no distraction, where there was a distance and a barrenness that built up to a vast impersonality which emphasized and underscored the inconsequence of the thinker. For if the thinker introduced himself as a factor out of proportion to the fact, then the whole problem was distorted and the equation, if equation there be, never could be solved.

AT FIRST he had tried to hunt animals for food, but strangely, while the rest of the wilderness swarmed with vicious life that hunted timid life, the area around the city was virtually deserted, as if some one had drawn a sacred chalk mark around it. On his second day of hunting he killed a small thing that on Earth could have been a mouse. He built a fire and cooked it and later hunted up the sun-dried skin and sucked and chewed at it for the small nourishment that it might contain. But after that he did not kill a thing, for there was nothing to be killed.

Finally he came to know the seven would not come, that they never had intended to come, that they had deserted him exactly as his two human companions had deserted him before. He had been made a fool, he knew, not once, but twice.

He should have kept on going east after he had started. He should not have come back with seven to find the other six who waited at the canyon's mouth.

You might have made it to the settlements, he told himself.

You just might have made it. Just possibly have made it.

East. East toward the settlements.

Human history is a trying...a trying for the impossible, and attaining it. There is no logic, for if humanity had waited upon logic it still would be a cave-lining and an earth-bound race.

"Try," said Webb, not knowing exactly what he said.

He walked down the hill again and started out across the wilderness, heading toward the east. For there was no hope upon the hill and there was hope toward the east.

A mile from the base of the hill he fell. He staggered, falling and rising, for another mile. He crawled a hundred yards. It was there the seven found him.

"Food!" he cried at them and he had a feeling that although he cried it in his mind there was no sound in his mouth. "Food! Water!"

"We take care," they said, and lifted him, holding him in a sitting position.

"Life," Seven told him, "is in many husks. Like nested boxes that fit inside each other. You live one and you peel it off and there's another life."

"Wrong," said Webb. "You do not talk like that. Your thought does not flow like that. There is something wrong."

"There is an inner man," said Seven. "There are many inner men."

"The subconscious," said Webb and while he said it in his mind, he knew that no word, no sound came out of his mouth. And he knew now, too, that no words were coming out of Seven's mouth, that here were words that could not be expressed in the patois of the desert, that here were thoughts and knowledge that could not belong to a thing that scuttled, fearsome, through the Martian wilderness.

"You peel an old life off and you step forth in a new and shining life," said Seven, "but you must know the way. There is a certain technique and a certain preparation. If there is no preparation and no technique, the job is often bungled."

"Preparation," said Webb. "I have no preparation. I do not

know about this."

"You are prepared," said Seven. "You were not before, but now you are."

"I thought," said Webb.

"You thought," said Seven, "and you found a partial answer. Well-fed, earth-bound, arrogant, there would have been no answer. You found humility."

"I do not know the technique," said Webb. "I do not..."

"We know the technique," Seven said. "We take care."

The hilltop where the dead city lay shimmered and there was a mirage on it. Out of the dead mound of its dust rose the pinnacles and spires, the buttresses and the flying bridges of a city that shone with color and with light; out of the sand came the blaze of garden beds of flowers and the tall avenues of trees and a music that came from the slender bell towers.

There was grass beneath his feet instead of sand blazing with the heat of the Martian noon. There was a path that led up the terraces of the hill toward the wonder city that reared upon its heights. There was the distant sound of laughter and there were flecks of color moving on the distant streets and along the walls and through the garden paths.

Webb swung around and the seven were not there. Nor was the wilderness. The land stretched away on every hand and it was not wilderness, but a breath-taking place with groves of trees and roads and flowing watercourses.

He turned back to the city again and watched the movement of the flecks of color.

"People," he said.

And Seven's voice, coming to him from somewhere, from elsewhere, said:

"People from the many planets. And from beyond the planets. And some of your own people you will find among them. For you are not the first."

Filled with wonder, a wonder that was fading, that would be entirely faded before he reached the city, Webb started walking up the path.

WAMPUS SMITH and Lars Nelson came to the hill many days late. They came on foot because the wilderness wagon had broken down. They came without food except the little food they could kill along the way and they came with no more than a few drops of water sloshing in their canteens and there was no water to be found.

There, a short distance from the foot of the hill, they found the sun-dried mummy of a man face downward on the sand and when they turned him over they saw who he was.

Wampus stared across the body at Lars.

"How did he get here?" he croaked.

"I don't know," said Lars. "He never could have made it, not knowing the country and on foot. And he wouldn't have traveled this way anyhow. He would have headed east, back to the settlements."

They pawed through his clothing and found nothing. But they took his gun, for the charges in their own were running very low.

"What's the use," said Lars. "We can't make it, Wampus."

"We can try," said Wampus.

Above the hill a mirage flickered...a city with shining turrets and dizzy pinnacles and rows of trees and fountains that flashed with leaping water. To their ears came the sound, or seemed to come, the sound of many bells.

Wampus spat with lips that were cracked and dried, spat with no saliva in his mouth.

"Damn mirages," he said. "They drive a man half crazy."

"They seem so close," said Lars. "So close and real. As if they were someplace else and were trying to break through."

Wampus spat again. "Let's get going," he said.

The two men turned toward the east and as they moved, they left staggering, uneven tracks through the sand of Mars.

THE END

Quarantined Species

By
J. F. BONE

Those Venusian horgels were cute, clever, intelligent. They made perfect pets. They were lovable. — But that was the big trouble. They were much, much too lovable!

"DID you ever own a cat?" Thompson asked. He leaned forward, a small gray man in his late sixties, and peered at his visitor through old-fashioned bifocals across the breadth of desk which separated them. The young man standing before the desk fidgeted impatiently as Thompson looked down at the interview card which read "Edward Farnsworth—Agent, Worldwide Shows", and scratched the ears of the big Siamese cat sitting on his lap. The cat looked up with incurious blue eyes, regarded Farnsworth with a peculiarly dispassionate stare, stretched, yawned, and closed his eyes again. It was perfectly apparent that the tall swarthy visitor was a matter of complete disinterest. "Now take Cato, here," Thompson continued. "He's a fine specimen of a cat. Have you owned anything like him?"

"Once," Farnsworth said, "when I went to Venus. But I don't see what this has to do with my business with you. All I want is a simple answer. Do I or do I not get permission to import a pair of Venusian horgels?"

"You do not," Thompson said succinctly.

"This makes the fourth time," Farnsworth sighed. "So I'll have to go to higher authority, I suppose."

"There is no higher authority, son. This is the end of the line."

"You bureaucrats!" Farnsworth's voice was filled with poorly suppressed anger. "You sit here behind a desk and play God! Tell us working people what they can and can't do just as though you knew all the answers, and never give a tinker's dam about the fact that your stupid decisions can ruin people. Just why in heaven's name won't you allow something cute and clever like the horgels to be brought to Earth? There's nothing wrong with them. They'll survive nicely in a terrestrial environment. —and they'll save our show from bankruptcy. People will simply love them if they're given a chance."

"I suppose they would," Thompson said, "but I doubt if they'll ever get a chance to do it. They're a quarantined species." There was an odd note of grimness in his voice. "Cat's don't like them," he added obliquely.

"What's that got to do with it?"

"I repeat—have you ever owned a cat?"

"And I repeat, sir, I did. It was mandatory to own one on Venus—although why it was, God only knows. There are millions of cats there, and to require a man to lead a Siamese around on a leash is sheer foolishness!"

"You're like all the rest," Thompson sighed. "You confuse words with facts. You never owned a cat in your life."

"But—"

"You just think you did," Thompson concluded gently.

"I have papers to prove it!'

"So what? Did your cat ever obey you when it didn't wish to? Did it ever sacrifice its comfort for your own? Did it ever go out of its way to be good to you?"

Farnsworth shook his head. "I can't say that it did," he admitted. "It was a nasty selfish brute. I loathe cats!"

"But you like horgels."

"Yes—I'm quite fond of them. They're cute, and clever,

—and loveable."

"Hmp! Yes—they are. That's the trouble with them. They're *too* cute, *too* clever, and *too* loveable!"

"That's impossible!"

"That so? — Just a moment son. How long were you around those horgels?"

"Just a few days. A swamprat owned them. Kept them in a locked cage and never touched them. He even had one of the natives feed them. The poor little things were terrified. I don't think they'd ever been in a cage before, and I can't see why they were. They're the softest most endearing things. They'd make perfect pets."

"Undoubtedly they would," Thompson said. "Well, there's no damage done. Oh, by the way, did you see any cats about the place?"

"No—none but my own—I heard them. Nasty brutes that yowled all night."

"That's one worry taken care of. I was afraid that I'd have to ask you where that trader lived, and I know you wouldn't tell me. Thompson beamed pleasantly at him over his spectacles. "The cats will take care of them. It's just a matter of time."

"You mean that they'll kill those inoffensive little things?"

"Of course. It's a matter of priority rights." There was iron in Thompson's voice. "Cat's are great believers in direct action. Now sit down, young man and I'll tell you why you'll never get an entry permit from this office, and why you'll never again be allowed to visit Venus."

"But you can't do that!"

"I already have," Thompson said gently. "I revoked your ship permit before I ever saw you."

"You what?"

"You heard me son. Venus is closed."

"But why?"

"Sit down and I'll tell you."

Farnsworth sputtered, but did what he was told. At least, he reflected bitterly, he should get something out of this highly unsatisfactory interview.

"THAT'S fine," Thompson beamed. "There's nothing like acquiring knowledge. And the first bit of knowledge you should acquire is that I haven't always been a bureaucrat. Once I was a biotechnician in the Space Service, and I was a member of the first expedition to Venus. There were five of us on the "Venus I". Archie Slezak the pilot, Ed Smith the navigator, Mitsui Watanabe the engineer, and myself. And then there was Katy, the ship's cat.

"She was an unlisted crewmember, a big, black, short-haired cat of dubious ancestry. From her size, I'd judge that there was a little wildcat somewhere in her family tree, but despite the fact that she looked like a black panther, she was affectionate enough in her way, and we all endured her—all except Watanabe. He liked her. I think he smuggled her aboard before we took off even though he never admitted it. He was a sucker for pets. But she never paid too much attention to him. Generally she was nosing around in dark corners of the ship once acceleration pressure was off.

"We had a little artificial gravity of course, but it was about one eighth Earth normal, just enough to keep our feet. Katy loved it. It was nothing for her to leap twenty feet across the control room, and land on one of our shoulders, so lightly that we hardly felt her. She had an incredible judgment of distance, and would amuse us by the hour with her antics.

"As far as cats went, she was likeable enough, but I never really trusted her. There was a little too much of the wildcat in her," he reached down and scratched Cato's ears and smiled when the big tom swore at him in low Siamese.

"Then why—" Farnsworth began.

"Save it son—I'll explain. As I was saying, we all thought she was amusing but useless until the day she came floating into the control room with a dead rat in her jaws. It was a pregnant female filled with pups, and I'll tell you it scared us silly!

"Rats and spaceships just don't go together. They breed fast and mutate easily in the drive radiations, and once they get started they're hard to control. It's particularly bad if an intelligent mutation appears, but Katy stopped that threat before it ever got started.

"We got into spacesuits and blew the ship down. Not even rats can live in a vacuum, and we kept the ship open long enough to make sure the last trace of air was removed from the fiberglass insulation of the hull. Fortunately, none of our unwanted guests had been exposed to the drive radiations long enough for mutations to appear, so we managed to get a complete kill. Watanabe had fixed a pressure tank for Katy, and during the blowdown she sat in it as smug as a dowager empress while we killed off the rats.

"After that, Katy was a heroine. And did she take advantage of it! It was almost as though she knew she had reached privileged status. She'd boss us around, and glare at us to move if we were sitting on one of her favorite spots. She wasn't very nice about it, and if you've been bossed by a cat you'll understand what I mean.

"She liked to be petted, but wanted affection on her own terms and time, and she picked the damndest times. Whenever Smitty was busy with calculations, there would be Katy sitting in the middle of his papers, tail straight up in the air, her back arched, and her purr as loud as a dynamotor. And when I checked the algae tanks for ecological balance, there she'd be trying to unbalance the ecology. And if Mitsui wanted to check the engines he always had to check the cat first. She was a pest.

"But poor Slezak got it worst. For some unknown reason Katy liked him—and Archie hated cats. She'd fuss over him, croon cat talk to him, and then slump bonelessly on his lap and sleep.

"Archie's body temperature probably had a lot to do with it, since it was a full degree warmer than the rest of ours, but Slezak used to say that she did it deliberately out of sheer orneriness—and I wouldn't disagree with him.

"Anything was possible where Katy was concerned. She looked on the ship and all that was in it as her personal property, especially created for her comfort and amusement, and she used it just that way. There was something direct about her that didn't bother with such niceties as form and attitude. She was a cat—we were only human—and she was never averse to putting us in our place.

"WE spent two months coasting under minimum power, and then started the braking run. We blasted down after turnover until we got the trajectory straightened out, and then let Venus do the rest. We circled the planet just above the ion belt where the few molecules of atmosphere slowed us down without too much overheating, making close range observations of the world below.

"We checked the atmosphere. The upper layer was mainly carbon dioxide and formaldehyde, just like the astronomy boys said it would be, but it was neither thick nor cloudy. The clouds were all down at the surface. As you know, Venus has a heavy-gas based atmosphere, but even then the oxygen content was high, enough to be breathable if you didn't mind the smell of embalming fluid.

"Our orders called for landing if it was feasible, so Slezak cleared the board and trimmed ship for a setdown. We made it all right, and landed on one of those humps of land that stick up out of the swamp. There wasn't much to see, of course. Venus was a pretty dismal place what with the steady rain and air that smelled like a cut-rate undertaking parlor. But I shouldn't have to tell you what Venus is like. You've been there too."

"It still is bad," Farnsworth said. "It hasn't improved much."

"Any improvement in Venus would be a lot," Thompson continued. "Well, we did the usual things—planted the flag and claimed the planet, and then while Slezak and I stayed with the ship, Smitty and Watanabe went exploring. We drew straws for the honor, and Archie and I won.

"We stayed close to the ship, peering through the rain for what seemed hours, walking around a little and stretching our legs. We weren't equipped for any real exploration work but we had to do some to make the claim legal. The real work would come later, after the lads back home evaluated our data, but at least we had the honor of being the first humans to set foot on the planet." Thompson coughed rackingly and smiled when the spasm passed. "The memory still gets me," he explained. "I never could stand formaldehyde. My lungs got over being partially embalmed years ago, but thinking of Venus still makes me cough.

"IT was about an hour before Smitty and Mitsui came back. Mitsui had a horgel in his arms. The kid was a sucker for animals, but this time we all thought he really had something. None of us had ever seen a horgel before, and it looked so innocent and appealing that we couldn't help falling for it.

"With its pink fur and violet eyes it looked for all the world like a child's doll, a pint-sized teddy bear with a button nose, black, handlike feet, and an expression of utter trust on its pointed face. But that didn't explain all of its appeal. I guess there is a little of the mother in every man, because the damn thing touched something within us that could only be called the maternal instinct. There's nothing else that can describe it. It made us feel all soft inside, and everyone of us wanted to hold it and protect it."

"I know," Farnsworth said. "I've held one."

"Mitsui had fallen in love with it. You know how emotional the Japanese are. He was cuddling it in his arms and whispering sweet words into its shell-like ears, and it was crooning back at him. His actions would have made me sick except that I wanted to hold it so bad that it hurt. I wanted to feel the softness of its fur, to pet and fondle it. I wanted it like I'd want a woman. Smitty was green with jealousy and even Slezak looked interested. All of us were acting a little queer. I suppose, but it seemed all right at the time.

"Katy didn't react like we did. She came to the entrance port, stepping delicately as though she was treading on eggs and was afraid of breaking them—but the moment she saw the little pink puffball in Watanabe's arms her whole attitude changed. Her back arched and her tail looked like a bottle brush! She let out one yowl of pure hate and leaped for Mitsui! Her claws dug into his jacket as she clawed upward toward the horgel, a screaming, spitting fury of insane rage!

"The horgel screamed just once. It sounded so much like a hurt baby that we were paralyzed for a moment—and while we were all standing there, it leaped from Mitsui's arms and ran clumsily across the seared landing area to the jungle some fifty yards away. But it never reached it. Katy was after it like a thunderbolt! She caught it after it had gone about twenty yards, and by the time we reached the scene, she had swiftly and completely demolished it.

"Now, I've seen cats kill many times, but it always seemed to be more for the fun of it than anything else. Cats appear to hunt for the sport of the thing, but there was no sport in

Katy. She simply caught the horgel and tore it to ribbons!

"Mitsui was heartbroken. From the way he acted it was almost as though Katy had killed his baby brother. 'I loved that little thing!' he sobbed. 'I've never seen anything so trusting and affectionate. Oh! *damn* that dirty cat!'

"I cocked an interested ear. Mitsui was always the one who had defended Katy. He always liked her—wasted three times the affection on her than any of the rest of us did. But right now he would have cheerfully killed her. Katy apparently realized how he felt, because she beat a quick retreat to the ship and hid in one of the dark corners she knew so well, while Mitsui prowled after her calling the wrath of his Japanese ancestors down upon her murderous head. Katy, of course, ignored him.

"Mitsui calmed down after an hour or so, but he spent the rest of the evening building a strong box with a barred door. 'It's not that I don't like Katy,' he said apologetically. 'But I loved that little thing.'

"He waited patiently until Katy came out of hiding, scooped her up and popped her suprised body into the box. 'Now stay there until you can learn to behave yourself,' he said grimly. Then without a word to us he walked outside and in a half-hour came back with another of the pink things exactly like the one he had lost. He was grinning from ear to ear. 'There's a village over there,' he said pointing outside the port, 'and these animals are as thick as fleas on a dog's back. The natives keep them for pets.'

"So Mitsui Watanabe was the first one of us to discover the dominant intelligence of Venus. But we weren't thinking of that. We just wanted one of those delightful creatures for our own. And this time there was no drawing straws. We set out in a body, leaving a raging Katy behind us safely locked up in the box.

"THE village was a cluster of mud huts filled with little humanoid natives. You know what they're like—stupid, imitative primitives who follow you around looking for something to beg or steal. I understand that they're no different now than they were.

"The only difference was that the village simply swarmed with horgels. They were everywhere, scampering familiarly through the village for all the world like a lot of pet dogs.

"As far as we could tell, the humanoids were a harmless lot. From what we could see, they spent their time fishing and taking care of their pets and children. The way they coddled those pink furballs was amazing. I even saw nursing mothers feed them at the same breast they fed their children! It was a perfect expression of the love and tenderness the horgels inspired.

"The natives didn't object when we scooped up a horgel apiece and held them in our arms. There were plenty of them and they seemed to be community property. The horgels apparently liked us as much as we liked them, because it was no time at all before we were all acting like kids despite our space ratings, and since you've held a horgel you know how we felt."

Farnsworth nodded. "They are appealing," he said. "I never experienced a sensation quite like holding one of them. There's no word for it."

"Sure there is, son. Try *love*." Thompson's voice softened and then turned cynical. "Anyway, we took them back to the ship with us, and Katy went crazy in her box. She swore, snarled, screamed, spat and clawed until she was exhausted, and then lay on the bottom of the box and growled at us. It wasn't a nice noise but it did her no good. The box would have held a bobcat. And we weren't listening.

"We were fascinated by the horgels. They were

111

wonderful, —soft, clever, affectionate and intelligent too. Mitsui taught his to sit up in a matter of minutes, and for hours afterwards we explored their repertoire of accomplishments.

"They could do almost everything but talk—and they could darn near do that. They seemed to know instinctively what we wanted—and what would please us most—and then they did that thing. It was a happy time for all of us. We never had so much fun simply watching the antics of our new found pets. They were natural comedians, and kept us laughing most of the night. And when we finally turned in, each of us held his horgel in his arms.

"And no one remembered to feed Katy.

"It probably would have done no good if we had, since she was so mad that she would have refused food. And her disposition didn't improve. But we didn't forget her completely—after a day or so we gave her food and left her alone. If she wanted to eat—all right. Otherwise we didn't care. Being a cat, and being sensible, she ate. But there was no gratitude or affection for our kindness. She just crouched in the back of the box and spat at us.

"WE spent several days on the island in the swamp, but found nothing of interest outside of the natives and the horgels. We took pictures, made notes, and tried to make some sense out of that perfectly incomprehensible native language. But about the only thing we learned was the name of the pink creatures and that everybody loved them.

"Of course we had to take off sooner than we would like, but Venus was passing conjunction, and if we waited too long our fuel supply wouldn't take us back to Earth. So we loaded our horgels and ourselves into the ship, blasted off for Earth, and bade farewell to the formaldehyde stink of Venus' air.

"We were a week out, and had built up to terminal velocity

when it happened. Somehow Katy managed to open her cage and escape. The first I knew about it was when she killed my horgel—bit through its spine as it lay sleeping on my bed. She was so quiet that I never knew what had happened until I woke to find my poor little puffball lying cold and stiff in the circle of my arm.

"I looked for the cat all the next period, and every free chance I had thereafter. I wanted to kill her. Losing my horgel was just like losing a child! I was disconsolate—and consumed with envy for my more fortunate crewmembers. Their horgels were still alive and mine was dead! And my companions were utterly selfish! They must have known how I felt, but they wouldn't share their horgels with me for a moment. I felt like a single man on a desert island peopled by happy and contented couples. I was left out—and I was miserable!

"It's odd how the horgels took on the attributes of all the desirable women I had longed for but never had. The loss of my pet and the obvious callousness of my companions to my feelings made the sense of loss even more sharp than it would have been otherwise. I took it badly. At first I was hurt and miserable. But gradually I began to hate the others for their good fortune, their cruel selfishness, their lack of consideration. And finally my thoughts turned toward murder.

"What right did these others have to possess horgels when I had none? I brooded about it during the days we sped Earthward. I was damned if they were going to have all the pleasures of companionship while I was left out in the cold.

"I thought it over carefully, and finally decided that Smitty was the one who would least be missed. I waylaid him in the passageway that period, and damn near fractured his skull with a wrench. He dropped to the deck, blood streaming from his head—but I didn't give him a thought until I had his horgel. Once I had that pink puffball safe in my arms, I felt sorry for him and carted him up to his shockcouch where I patched up his injuries as best I could. But I didn't give up the horgel.

"Peculiarly enough, none of the others seemed the least shocked at what I had done. As long as it was for a horgel, and since the horgel wasn't theirs, it was all right. But as Smitty improved, I began to fear that he would try to take it back, and that, I swore grimly, would never happen. The pet I had stolen was just as precious as the one I had lost —and I wouldn't trade the world for it. It was my joy and pleasure, and I guarded it fiercely from harm.

"I couldn't forget Katy and her hatred for the creatures, and that cat was still loose, roaming somewhere through the ship looking for more horgels to kill. But I didn't search for her. I wasn't going to take any chances on losing my pet. Instead I stayed in the open where it was safe—and carried the wrench with which I'd nearly brained Smitty. It wasn't for Katy alone. I was equally afraid that Smitty would try to take the horgel back from me once he recovered.

"But I needn't have wasted the energy. As the days passed and there was no sign of Katy, our vigilance relaxed, and the horgels didn't like to be held all the time. They were active little things who liked to romp.

"So we finally gave in and allowed them the freedom of the control room, after searching it carefully, of course. There they would tumble and play with each other while we watched with fondly possessive eyes. Smitty looked at them from his shockcouch where he lay with his head bandaged— and his eyes were murderous when he looked at me. I knew what was passing through his mind, and in a strange sort of way I sympathized with him, but a pet like the horgel was worth all the hate Smitty could generate. I felt good. I had a pet and he didn't.

"IT was then that Katy struck! She must have been waiting with devilish patience for her opportunity, because when Mitsui opened the door to go aft to inspect the drives, she darted in.

"A sweep of her claws disemboweled the closest of the fragile little creatures, and with a leap and pounce she seized the other in her jaws and disappeared down through the door in one of those long swift leaps that she had perfected on the outward voyage. It was done so swiftly that neither Slezak nor I had time to move. Mitsui had time only for a startled curse as Katy sailed down the shaft toward the stern with the heart-rending scream of the horgel following her. It died to a choked whimper as she disappeared.

"We found the torn pink body in the drive room a few minutes later but there was no sign of Katy.

"But now instead of three horgels and four men, there was one horgel and four men.

"Slezak and I stood it for a week until we made an agreement based on desperation and loss. We would take the last horgel from Mitsui and share it between ourselves. If we had to kill Mitsui to get it, well, that was his bad luck.

"We shook hands on it, but I knew from the look in his eye that he didn't intend to keep his promise. I had enough of broken promises—so I decided to kill him after we had disposed of Mitsui. Then I would kill Smitty and have the delightful creature all to myself without anyone to bother my enjoyment. And I'd never give Katy another chance.

"It was all perfectly logical. After all, there was only one horgel and it should belong to the one who could best take care of it. I was obviously the one since I had lost two already and was fully conscious of the menace Katy represented.

"But it was hard to catch Mitsui off guard. He went around with the horgel buttoned under his jacket and a loaded pistol in his pocket. Apparently he'd smuggled the gun aboard in defiance of the regulation which prohibited side-arms aboard ship. He said it was for Katy, but Slezak and I knew better. We knew the gun was for us if we tried to take the horgel from him. It made us cautious.

"Much as we wanted that loveable little creature, we didn't want to die for it. There could be no enjoyment of its charm if we were dead. And we couldn't carry rifles. Even if we could have stood up to their recoil in one eighth G they were too big and clumsy to carry in the cramped quarter of the ship.

"It was a weird situation, one that might have been laughable except for its deadly undertones. Smitty recovered enough to walk around and naturally joined forces with us have-nots. He was still pretty weak, but any help lessened the odds. However I was always conscious of the speculative look in his eye when he looked at me.

"I would have to get rid of Smitty permanently after we had gotten Mitsui's pet or he would join forces with Slezak to murder me. I caught them whispering together once or twice, and the guilty looks they gave me were enough proof of their intentions. But none of us wanted to brave Mitsui's gun.

"IT stayed that way for nearly a week. We were just entering Earth's atmosphere, and Mitsui was busy with the engines when we made our bid. I jumped him from behind, while Slezak and Smith took him from the side.

"But I had forgotten that a Jap knows jiu jitsu like we know boxing. He bent—and suddenly I was flying over his head. I landed with a thump that knocked the breath out of me. I was sick and paralyzed with the shock, but I saw with satisfaction that Slezak had gotten the engineer's gun.

"But Mitsui wasn't through yet. He caught Smith with a

judo blow that almost tore his head off, and turned on Slezak, a squatty bronze fury with death in his hands. Slezak didn't even have time to raise the gun.

"But the fight had ripped Mitsui's jacket open and the horgel fell from the torn cloth. With a howl of terror, Mitsui bent to pick up the pink furred creature. Slezak's gunbarrel landed on the back of his head with crushing force before any of us saw what had caused him to cry out. And Katy leaped from behind a motor mount, snatched the horgel from Archie's clutching hands and killed it with one quick bite!

"Completely disregarding Slezak's anguished cry, she clawed and ripped the thing to bloody ribbons, and then arched her back and spat at him as if to say 'well, I've killed the last of the little monsters—now what are you going to do about it?'

"Slezak bent over and picked the cat up almost tenderly, turned—and smashed her head against the bulkhead with a full armed blow that would have killed a horse! Then he got down on his knees and picked at the bloody shreds of the horgel and cried like a baby.

"SOMEHOW or other we managed to get the ship down, but when the reception committee met us, their congratulations turned to stares of horror. Of course they found out what happened, and the next expedition to Venus instead of carrying explorers carried cats—a couple of hundred of them. The ship marked the landing site carefully, released the cats and came home. After that we sent exploration parties—and we've been operating like that ever since. It's been better than forty years now that we've been trying to clean up that planet—and we're obviously not through yet."

"Did you ever go back to Venus to see what your cats have done?" Farnsworth asked.

Thompson shook his head. "No," he admitted. "I never

returned. I didn't have the heart to," he added. "I like horgels too. But as long as I'm a few million miles away, it isn't so bad. I can even be philosophical about it. But up there, feeling as I feel and knowing what I know it'd drive me mad!

"Incidentally, Farnsworth, that's the reason you're grounded. Now that you know that we are methodically exterminating the horgels, Venus is no longer a safe place for you to be. The Government strangely enough, worries about the welfare of its citizens, and has no desire to see him in physical or mental danger when it isn't necessary. Since you've already held one of the horgels, you're no longer a safe risk. You're conditioned!"

Farnsworth's protest was ignored as Thompson swept on, speaking rapidly to forestall any possible interruption. "You see, the smart boys found out what the trouble was. Horgels are a menace. We never looked at them the right way. Instead of us owning the horgels, it was the other way around. –and they were greedy. They didn't want one man, they wanted all men! On Earth, an animal like that would be more disruptive than the Atom War. What that last one on the ship did to us was only a small sample of what they could do here if given a chance." Thompson shivered. "We missed that only because of Katy."

"But why did the cat hate them so?" Farnsworth asked curiously.

Thompson sighed and rose to his feet, dislodging Cato who jumped lithely to the floor voicing his disapproval. He looked down at the cat and smiled. "You may think you own me, old boy—but what you think and what I think are two different things." He faced Farnsworth and answered slowly. "As regards your question, there are two possible answers. The biologists say it's because of the horgel's body odor—it's sort of the reverse of catnip in its effect. But I think they're wrong. I think it's more basic than that. You see, like I said, you don't own a cat. The cat owns you—and those things were cutting in—violating Katy's prior rights. Katy had been queen of the ship, and she couldn't stand competition—for which the human race should be forever grateful."

THE END

Living Space

By
ISAAC ASIMOV

*Having mastered probability lanes, man found an indefinite number
of Earths—and everyone could have a planet all to himself, if he wanted.
But there was one joker in the deal...*

CLARENCE RIMBRO had no objections to living in the
only house on an uninhabited planet, anymore than had any
other of Earth's even trillion of inhabitants.

If someone had questioned him concerning possible objections, he would undoubtedly have stared blankly at the
questioner. His house was much larger than any house could
possibly be on Earth-proper, and much more modern. It had
its independent air-supply and water supply; ample food in its
freezing compartments. It was isolated from the lifeless
planet on which it was located by a force field, but the rooms
were built about a five-acre farm (under glass, of course)
which, in the planet's beneficent sunlight grew flowers for
pleasure and vegetables for health. It even supported a, few
chickens. It gave Mrs. Rimbro something to do with herself
afternoons, and a place for the two little Rimbros to play
when they were tired of indoors.

Furthermore, if one *wanted* to be on Earth-proper; if one
insisted on it; if one *had* to have people around, and air one
could breathe in the open, or water to swim in—one had only
to go out of the front door of the house.

So where was the difficulty?

Remember, too, that on the lifeless planet on which the
Rimbro house was located there was complete silence except
for the occasional monotonous effects of wind and rain.

There was absolute privacy and the feeling of absolute ownership of two hundred million square miles of planetary surface.

CLARENCE RIMBRO appreciated all that in his distant way. He was an accountant, skilled in handling very advanced computer models; precise in his manners and clothing; not given much to smiling beneath his thin, well-kept mustache; and properly aware of his own worth. When he drove from work toward home he passed the occasional dwelling-place on Earth-proper and he never ceased to stare at them with certain smugness.

Well, either for business reasons or due to mental perversion, some people simply had to live on Earth-proper. It was too bad for them. After all, Earth-proper's soil had to supply the minerals and basic food supply for all the trillion of inhabitants (in fifty years, it would be two trillion) and space was at a premium. Houses on Earth-proper just *couldn't* be any bigger than that; and people who had to live in them had to adjust to the fact.

Even the process of entering his house had its mild pleasantness. Rimbro would enter the community twist-place to which he was assigned (it looked, as did all such, like a rather stumpy obelisk) and there he would invariably find others waiting to use it. Still more would arrive before he reached the head of the line. It was a sociable time.

"How's your planet?" "How's yours?" The usual small talk. Sometimes someone would be having, trouble—machinery breakdowns, or serious weather that would alter the terrain unfavorably. Not often.

But conversational cliches passed the time; then Rimbro would be at the head of the line. He would put his key into the slot; the proper combination would be punched; and he would be twisted into a new probability pattern—his own particular probability pattern. This was the one assigned him when he married and became a producing citizen—a probability pattern in which life had never developed on Earth. And twisting to this particular lifeless Earth, he would walk into his own foyer.

Just like that.

RIMBRO NEVER worried about being in another probability; why should he? He never gave it any thought. There were an infinite number of possible Earths, and each existed in its own niche, its own probability pattern. Since on a planet such as Earth, there was—according to calculation—about a fifty-fifty chance of life's developing, half of all the possible Earths (still infinite, since half of infinity was infinity) possessed life, and half (still infinite) did not. And living on about three hundred billion families, each with its own beautiful house, powered by the sun of that probability, and each securely at peace. The number of Earths so occupied grew by millions each day.

And then one day, Rimbro came home and Sandra (his wife) said to him, as he entered, "There's been the most peculiar noise."

Rimbro's eyebrows shot up and he looked closely at his wife. Except for a certain restlessness of her thin hands and a pale look about the corners of her tight mouth, she looked normal.

Rimbro said, still holding his topcoat halfway toward the servette that waited patiently for it, "Noise? What noise? I don't hear anything."

"It's stopped now," Sandra said. "Really, it was like a deep thumping or rumble. You'd hear it a bit, then it would stop. Then you'd hear it a bit, and so on. I've never heard anything like it."

Rimbro surrendered his coat. "But that's quite impossible."

"I *heard* it."

"I'll look over the machinery," he mumbled. "Something may be wrong."

NOTHING was wrong that his accountant's eyes could discover and, with a shrug, Rimbro went to supper. He listened to the servettes hum busily about their different chores, watched one sweep up the plates and cutlery for disposal and recovery, then said, pursing his lips, "Maybe one of the servettes is out of order. I'll check them."

"It wasn't anything like that, Clarence."

Rimbro went to bed, without further concern over the matter—and wakened with his wife's hand clutching his shoulder. His hand went automatically to the contact-patch that set the walls glowing. "What's the matter? What time is it?"

She shook her head. "Listen! *Listen!*"

Good Lord, thought Rimbro, *there is a noise*. A definite rumbling; it came and went.

"Earthquake?" he whispered. Such things did happen, of course—though with all the planet to choose from, one could generally count on having avoided the faulted areas.

"All day long?" asked Sandra, fretfully. "I think it's something else." And then she voiced the secret terror of every nervous householder. "I think there's someone on the planet with us. This Earth is *inhabited.*"

Rimbro did the logical things. When morning came, he took his wife and children to his wife's mother. He himself took a day off and hurried to the Sector's housing Bureau.

He was quite annoyed at all this.

BILL CHING of the Housing Bureau was short, jovial, and proud of his part-Mongolian ancestry. He believed that probability patterns had solved every last one of humanity's problems. Alec Mishnoff, also of the Housing Bureau, thought probability patterns were a snare into which humanity had been hopelessly tempted. Mishnoff had originally majored in archeology, and had studied a variety of antiquarian subjects, with which his delicately poised head was still crammed. His face managed to look sensitive—despite overbearing eyebrows—and he lived with a pet notion that so far he had dared tell no one, though preoccupation with it had driven him out of archeology and into Housing.

Ching was fond of saying, "The hell with Malthus!" It was almost a verbal trademark of his, "The hell with Malthus; we can't possibly overpopulate now. However frequently we double and redouble, Homo sapiens remains finite in number, and the uninhabited Earths remain infinite. And we don't have to put one house on each planet; we can put a hundred, a thousand, a million. Plenty of room and plenty of power from each probability sun."

"More than one on a planet?" said Mishnoff, sourly.

Ching knew exactly what Alec meant. When probability patterns had first been put to use, sole ownership of a planet had been a powerful inducement for early settlers. It appealed to the snob and despot in everyone. What man so poor, ran the slogan, as not to have an empire larger than Genghis Khan's? To introduce multiple settling now would outrage everyone.

Ching said, with a shrug, "All right, it would take psychological preparation. So what? That's what it took to start the whole deal in the first place."

"And food?" asked Mishnoff.

"You know we're putting hydroponics works and yeast-plants in other probability patterns. And if we had to, we could cultivate their soil."

"Wearing space-suits and importing oxygen."

"We could reduce carbon dioxide for oxygen till the plants got going and they'd do the job after that."

"Given a million years."

"Mishnoff, the trouble with you," Ching said, "is that you read too many ancient history books. You're an obstructionist."

CHING WAS too good-natured really to mean that, and Mishnoff continued to read books and to worry. Mishnoff longed for the day he could get up the courage necessary to see the Head of the Section and put right out in plain view—bang, like that—exactly what it was that was troubling him.

But now a Mr. Clarence Rimbro faced them, perspiring slightly, and toweringly angry at the fact that it had taken him the better part of two days to reach this far into the Bureau.

He reached his exposition's climax by saying, "And I say the planet is inhabited and I don't propose to stand for it."

Having listened to his story in full, Ching tried the soothing approach. He said, "Noise like that is probably just some natural phenomenon."

"What kind of natural phenomenon?" demanded Rimbro. "I want an investigation. If it's a natural phenomenon, I want to know what kind. I say the place is inhabited; it has life on it, by heaven, and I'm not paying rent on a planet to share it. And with dinosaurs, from the sound of it."

"Come, Mr. Rimbro, how long have you lived on your Earth?"

"Fifteen and a half years."

"And has there ever been any evidence of life?"

"There is now, and as a citizen with a production record classified as A-1, I demand an investigation."

"Of course we'll investigate, sir; but we just want to assure you now that everything is all right. Do you realize how carefully we select our probability patterns?"

"I'm an accountant; I have a pretty good idea," said Rimbro at once.

"Then surely you know our computers cannot fail us. They never pick a probability that has been picked before; they can't possibly. And they're geared to select only probability patterns in which Earth has a carbon dioxide atmosphere, one in which plant life—and therefore animal life—has never developed. Because if plants had evolved, the carbon dioxide would have been reduced to oxygen. Do you understand?"

"I understand it all very well, and I'm not here for lectures," said Rimbro. "I want an investigation out of you, and nothing else. It is quite humiliating to think I may be sharing my world—my own world—with something or other; I don't propose to endure it."

"No, of course not," muttered Ching, avoiding Mishnoff's sardonic glance. "We'll be there before night."

THEY WERE on their way to the twisting-place with full equipment.

Mishnoff said, "I want to ask you something. Why do you go through that 'There's no need to worry, sir' routine? They always worry, anyway; where does it get you?"

"I've got to try. They *shouldn't* worry," said Ching, petulantly. "Ever hear of a carbon dioxide planet that was inhabited? Besides, Rimbro is the type that starts rumors; I can spot them. By the time he's through, if he's encouraged, he'll say his sun went nova."

"*That* happens sometimes," said Mishnoff.

"So? One house is wiped out and one family dies. See, you're an obstructionist. In the old times—the times you like—if there were a flood in China, or someplace, thousands of people would die. And that's out of a population of a measly billion or two."

Mishnoff muttered, "How do you know the Rimbro planet doesn't have life on it."

"Carbon dioxide atmosphere."

"But suppose—" It was no use; Mishnoff couldn't say it. He finished, lamely, "Suppose plant and animal life develops that can live on carbon dioxide."

"It's never been observed."

"In an infinite number of worlds, anything can happen." He finished that in a whisper, "Everything *must* happen."

"Chances are one in a duo-decillion," said Ching, shrugging.

They arrived at the twisting-point then, and having utilized the freight-twist for their vehicle (thus sending it into the Rimbro storage area) they entered the Rimbro probability pattern themselves. First Ching, then Mishnoff.

"A NICE house," said Ching, with satisfaction. "Very nice model; good taste."

"Hear anything?" asked Mishnoff.

"No."

Ching wandered into the garden. "Hey," he yelled, "Rhode Island Reds."

Mishnoff followed, looking up at the glass roof. The sun looked like the sun of a trillion other Earths.

He said, absently, "There could be plant life, just starting out. The carbon dioxide might just be starting to drop in concentration. The computer would never know."

"And it would take millions of years for animal life to begin and millions more for it to come out of the sea."

"It doesn't have to follow that pattern."

Ching put an arm about his partner's shoulder. "You brood. Some day, you'll tell me what's really bothering you, instead of just hinting; then we can straighten you out."

Mishnoff shrugged off the encircling arm with an annoyed

frown. Ching's tolerance was always hard to bear. He began, "Let's not psychotherapize—" He broke off then whispered, "Listen."

There was a distant rumble. Again.

THEY PLACED the seismograph in the center of the room, and activated the force field that penetrated downward and bound it rigidly to bedrock. They watched the quivering needle record the shocks.

Mishnoff said, "Surface waves only; very superficial. It's not underground."

Ching looked a little more dismal, "What is it then?"

"I think," said Mishnoff, "we'd better find out." His face was gray with apprehension. "We'll have to set up a seismograph at another point and get a fix on the focus of disturbance."

"Obviously," said Ching. "I'll go out with the other seismograph; you stay here."

"No," said Mishnoff, with energy. "I'll go out."

Mishnoff felt terrified, but he had no choice. If this were it, he would be prepared; he could get a warning through. Sending out an unsuspecting Ching could be disastrous. Nor could he warn Ching, who would certainly never believe him.

But since Mishnoff was not cast in the heroic mold, he trembled as he got into his oxygen suit and fumbled the disrupter, as he tried to dissolve the force field locally in order to free the emergency exit.

"Any reason *you* want to go, particularly?" asked Ching, watching the other's inept manipulations. "I'm willing."

"It's all right. I'm going out," said Mishnoff, out of a dry throat, and stepped into the lock that led out onto the desolate surface of a lifeless Earth. A presumably lifeless Earth.

THE SIGHT was not unfamiliar to Mishnoff; he had seen its like dozens of time. Bare rock, weathered by wind and rain, crusted and powdered with sand in the gullies; a small and noisy brook beating itself against its stony course. All brown and gray. No sign of green; no sound of life.

Yet, the sun was the same; and when night fell, the constellations would be the same.

The situation of the dwelling place was in that region which, on Earth-proper, would be called Labrador. (It was Labrador here, too, really. It had been calculated that in not more than one out of a quadrillion or so Earths were there significant changes in the geological development. The continents were everywhere recognizable down to quite small details.)

Despite the situation and the time of the year, which was October, the temperature was sticky warm due to the hothouse effect of the carbon dioxide in this Earth's dead atmosphere.

From inside his suit, through the transparent visor, Mishnoff watched it all somberly. If the epicenter of the noise were close by, adjusting the second seismograph a mile or so away would, be enough for the fix. If it weren't, they would have to bring in an air-scooter. Well, assume the lesser complication to begin with.

Methodically, he made his way up a rocky hillside. Once at the top, he could choose his spot.

Once at the top, puffing and feeling the heat most unpleasantly, he found he didn't have to.

His heart was pounding so that Mishnoff could scarcely hear his own voice as he yelled into his radio mouthpiece, "Hey, Ching, there's construction going on."

"What?" came back the appalled shout in his ears.

THERE WAS no mistake. Ground was being leveled;

machinery was at work; rock was being blasted out.

Mishnoff shouted, "They're blasting. That's the noise."

Ching called back, "But it's impossible. The computer would never pick the same probability pattern twice. *It couldn't.*"

"You don't understand—" began Mishnoff.

But Ching was following his own thought processes. "Get over there, Mishnoff. I'm coming out, too."

"No, damn it; you stay there," cried Mishnoff in alarm. "Keep me in radio contact, and for God's sake, be ready to leave for Earth-proper on wings if I give the word."

"Why?" demanded Ching. "What's going on?"

"I don't know yet," said Mishnoff; "give me a chance to find out."

To his own surprise, he noticed that his teeth were chattering.

Muttering breathless curses at the computer, at probability patterns, and at the insatiable need for living space on the part of a trillion human beings expanding in numbers like a puff of smoke, Mishnoff slithered and slipped down the other side of the slope, setting stones to rolling and rousing peculiar echoes.

A MAN came out to meet him, dressed in a gas-tight suit; different in many details from Mishnoff's own, but obviously intended for the same purpose—to lead oxygen to the lungs.

Mishnoff gasped breathlessly into his mouthpiece, "Hold it, Ching; there's a man coming. Keep in touch." Mishnoff felt his heart pump more easily and the bellows of his lungs labor less.

The two men were staring at one another. The other man was blond and craggy of face. The look of surprise about him was too extreme to be feigned.

He said, in a harsh voice, "*Wer sind Sie? Was machen Sie*

bier?"

Mishnoff was thunderstruck. He'd studied ancient German for two years in the days when he expected to be an archeologist; and he followed the comment, despite the fact that the pronunciation was not what he had been taught. The stranger was asking his identity and his business there.

Stupidly, Mishnoff stammered, *"Sprechen Sie Deutsch?"* and then had to mutter reassurance to Ching, whose agitated voice in his earpiece was demanding to know what the gibberish was all about.

The German-speaking one made no direct answer. He repeated, *"Wer sind Sie?"* and added impatiently, *"Hier ist fur ein narrischen Spass kein Zeit."*

Mishnoff didn't feel like a joke, either—particularly not a foolish one—but he continued, *"Spechen Sie Planetisch?"*

He did not know the German for "Planetary Standard Language" so he had to guess. Too late, he thought he should have refereed to it simply as English.

The other man stared wide-eyed at him. *"Sind Sie wahnsinnig?"*

Mishnoff was almost willing to settle for that; but in feeble self-defense, he said, "I'm not crazy, damn it. I mean, *Auf der Erde woher Sie ist gekcom—"*

He gave it up for lack of German, but the new idea that was rattling inside his skull would not quit its nagging. He had to find some way of testing it. He said, desperately, *"Welches Jahr ist es jetzt?"*

Presumably, the stranger—who was questioning his sanity already—would be convinced of Mishnoff's insanity now that he was being asked what year it was; but that was one question for which Mishnoff had the necessary German.

The other muttered something that sounded suspiciously like good German swearing and then said, *"Es ist doch drei-und-zwanzig vier-und-sechzig, und warum—"*

THE STREAM of German that followed was completely incomprehensible to Mishnoff; but in any case he had had enough for the moment. If he translated the German correctly, the year given him was 2364, which was nearly two thousand years in the past. How could that be?

He muttered, *"Drei-und-zwanzig vier-und-sechzig?"*

"Ja, ja," said the other with deep sarcasm. *"Drei-und-zwanzig vier-und-sechzig. Der ganze Jahr lang ist es so gewesen."*

Mishnoff shrugged. The statement that it had been so all year long was a feeble witticism—even in German—and it gained nothing in translation. He pondered.

But then, the other's ironical tone deepening, the German-speaking one went on. *"Drei-und-zwanzig vier-und-sechzig nach Hitler. Hilft das Ihnen veilleicht? Nach Hitler!"*

Mishnoff yelled with delight. "That *does* help me. *Es hilft! Horen Sie, bitte*—" He went on in broken German, interspersed with scraps of Planetary. "For heavens sake *um Gottes willen*—"

Making it 2364 after Hitler was different altogether.

He put German together desperately, trying to explain.

The other frowned and grew thoughtful. He lifted his gloved hand to stroke his chin, or make some equivalent gesture, hit the transparent visor that covered his face and left his hand there uselessly, while he thought.

He said, suddenly, *"Ich heiss George Fallenby."*

To Mishnoff it seemed that the name must be of Anglo-Saxon derivation, although the change in vowel form as pronounced by the other made it seem Teutonic.

"'Guten Tag," said Mishnoff, awkwardly, *"Ich heiss Alec Mishnoff,"* and was suddenly aware of the Slavic derivation of his own name.

"Kommen Sie mit mir, Herr Mishnoff," said Fallenby.

Mishnoff followed with a strained smile, muttering into his

transmitter. "It's all right Ching; it's all right."

BACK ON Earth-proper. Mishnoff faced the Sector's Bureau head, who had grown old in the Service; whose every gray hair betokened a problem met and solved; and every missing hair a problem averted. He was a cautious man with eyes still bright and teeth that were still his own. His name was Berg.

He shook his head. "And they speak German? But the German you studied was two thousand years old."

"True" said Mishnoff, "but the English that Hemingway used is two thousand years old and Planetary is close enough for anyone to be able to read it."

"Hmm. And who's this Hitler?"

"He was a sort of tribal chief in ancient times. He led the German tribe, in one of the wars of the twentieth century— just about the time the Atomic Age started, and true history began."

"Before the Devastation you mean?"

"Right. There were a series of wars then; the Anglo-Saxon countries won out and I suppose that's why the Earth speaks Planetary."

"And if Hitler and his Germans had won out the world would speak German instead?"

"They *have* won out on Fallenby's Earth, sir, and they *do* speak German."

"And make their dates 'after Hitler' instead of A. D.?"

"Right. And I suppose there's an Earth in which the Slavic tribes won out and everyone speaks Russian."

"Somehow," said Berg, "it seems to me we should have foreseen it; and yet as far as I know, no one has. After all, there are an infinite number of inhabited Earths; we can't be the only one that has decided to solve the problem of unlimited population growth by expanding into the worlds of probability"

"Exactly," said Mishnoff, earnestly, "and it seems to me that—if you think of it—there must be countless inhabited Earths so doing, and there must be many multiple occupations in the three hundred billion Earths we ourselves occupy. The only reason we caught this one is that, by sheer chance, they decided to build within a mile of the dwelling we had placed there. This is something we must check."

"You imply we ought to search all our Earths."

"I do, sir; we've got to make some settlement with other inhabited Earths. After all, there is room for all of us; to expand without agreement may result in all sorts of trouble and conflict."

"Yes," said Berg, thoughtfully; "I agree with you."

CLARENCE RIMBRO stared suspiciously at Berg's old face, creased now into all manner of benevolence. "You're sure now?"

"Absolutely," said the Sector Head, "We're sorry that you've had to accept temporary quarters for the last two weeks—"

"More like three."

"—three weeks, but you will be compensated."

"What was the noise?"

"Purely geological, sir. A rock was delicately balanced and with the wind, it made occasional contact with the rocks of the hillside. We've removed it and surveyed the area to make certain that nothing similar will occur again"

Rimbro clutched his hat and said, "Well, thanks for your trouble."

"No thanks necessary, I assure you, Mr. Rimbro. This is our job."

RIMBRO was ushered out and Berg turned to Mishnoff,

who had remained a quiet spectator of this completion of the Rimbro affair.

Berg said, "The Germans were nice about it, anyway. They admitted we had priority and got off. Room for everybody, they said. Of course, as it turned out, they build any number of dwellings on each unoccupied world. —And now there's the project of surveying our other worlds and making similar agreements with whomever we find. It's all strictly confidential, too. It can't be made known to the populace without plenty of preparation. —Still, none of this is what I want to speak to you about."

"Oh?" said Mishnoff. Developments had not noticeably cheered him; his own bogey still concerned him.

Berg smiled at the younger man. "You understand, Mishnoff, that we in the Bureau—and in the Planetary Government, too—are very appreciative of your quick thinking, of your understanding of the situation. This could have developed into something very tragic, had it not been for you. This appreciation will take some tangible form."

"Thank you, sir."

"But as I said once before, this is something many of us should have thought of. How is it you did? —Now we've gone into your background a little. Your coworker, Ching, tells us you have hinted in the past at some serious danger involved in our probability pattern setup, and that you insisted on going out to meet the Germans—although you were obviously frightened. You were anticipating what you actually found, were you not? How did you do it?"

Mishnoff said, confusedly. "No, no. That was not in my mind at all; it came as a surprise. I—"

SUDDENLY, he stiffened. Why not now? They were grateful to him. He had proved that he was a man to be taken into account; one unexpected thing had already happened.

He said, firmly, "There's something else."

"Yes?"

(How did one begin?) "There's no life in the Solar System other than the life on Earth."

"That's right," said Berg, benevolently.

"And computation has it that the probability of developing any form of interstellar travel is so low as to be infinitesimal."

"What are you getting at?"

"That all this is so *in this probability*! But there must be some probability patterns in which other life *does* exist in the Solar System, or in which interstellar drives are developed by dwellers in other star systems."

Berg frowned. "Theoretically."

"In one of these probabilities, Earth may be visited by such intelligences. If it were a probability pattern in which Earth is inhabited, it won't affect us; they'll have no connection with us in Earth-proper. But if it were a probability pattern in which Earth is uninhabited, and they set up some sort of base, they may find, by happenstance, one of our dwelling places."

"Why ours?" demanded Berg, dryly. "Why not a dwelling place of the Germans, for instance?"

"Because we spot our dwellings one to a world. The German Earth doesn't, and probably very few others do. The odds are in favor of us by billions to one. And if extra-terrestrials do find such a dwelling, they'll investigate and find the route to Earth-proper—a highly-developed, rich world."

"Not if we turn off the twisting-place," said Berg.

"ONCE THEY know that twisting-places exist, they can construct their own," said Mishnoff. "A race intelligent enough to travel through space could do that; and from the equipment in the dwelling they would take over, they could easily spot our particular probability. —And then how would we handle extra-terrestrials? They're not Germans, or other Earths; they would have alien psychologies and motivations. And we're not even on our guard. We just keep setting up more and more worlds and increasing the chance every day that—"

His voice had risen in excitement and Berg shouted at him, "Nonsense. This is all ridiculous—"

The buzzer sounded and the communiplate brightened, and showed the face of Ching. Ching's voice said, "I'm sorry to interrupt, but—"

"What is it?" demanded Berg, savagely.

"There's a man here I don't know what to do with. He's drunk or crazy; he complains that his home is surrounded, and that there are things staring through the glass-roof of his garden."

"Things?" cried Mishnoff.

"Purple things with big red veins, three eyes, and some sort of tentacles instead of hair. They have—"

But Mishnoff and Berg didn't hear the rest; they were staring at each other in sick horror.

THE END

Iron Man

By
EANDO BINDER

It was a new type of obsession for a psychotherapist—a man who was firmly convinced that he was a robot!

CHARLEY BECKER dropped his tools and announced, "I'm going to get oiled."

Hank Norton looked up in surprise at his co-worker in the sonox department. Becker was small and slight, with thin hair and the makings of a bald spot. He was the quiet kind who worked week in and week out with patient efficiency. He was inconspicuous, and sometimes you hardly knew he was there. It was hard not to smile at his thin voice that always came out like a woman's high-pitched treble.

That was partly what surprised Hank Norton. Becker's voice had come out in a deep manly tone, for once. More shocking were the words. As far as anybody knew, Charley Becker had never taken a drop in his life; two beers would have been a rip-roaring orgy for him.

"Did *you* say that, Charley?" Norton queried, just to be sure.

"Yes, I'm going to get oiled," Becker boomed again.

Norton nodded in understanding then, noting his strained face. "Shaky nerves, Charley? I've seen it happen before. Working year after year on these monotonous robot sonox units sure can get a guy at times."

He shot a spark into the speech center of the robot he was working on. The robot came to life and gave out an eerie, human-like groan. "Almost sounds human," Norton said. "Plenty weird, coming from a bunch of junk. Never thought

138

it would get you, though, Charley. It's only an hour to quitting time; keep working and forget it."

But Becker was already turning. "I'm going to get oiled," he repeated, and stalked over to Pete Osgood in the grease pit.

"Oil me," he said.

Osgood wasn't in a good humor. "Layoff, Charley; that one has whiskers on it."

"I am in need of oiling," said Becker, standing there stiffly. He raised his left arm slowly, rigidly. "Observe, sir. This shoulder joint sticks; oil it, please."

Osgood got sore. "Now listen here, Charley. For the last time, don't try to make a fool of me."

"But I need oiling," said Becker. "And that is your duty."

Osgood snatched up an oil can. "You asked for it, Charley," he said with a wicked grin. He squirted oil lavishly over Becker's left shoulder. It soaked into his shirt and dripped off his elbow.

"You're all oiled up now, X-88," Osgood roared, suddenly amused, waiting for Becker's dismay.

"Thank you, sir," said Becker, swinging his arm freely. "The shoulder joint is now working properly."

He turned on his heel precisely and strode heavily to the door. Pete Osgood dropped the oilcan as Hank Norton came up.

"Goshsakes," Osgood choked. "He wasn't kidding."

Charles Becker marched out of the building and down the street along which sprawled the *Winton Robot Works*.

LORA BECKER was rearranging furniture, as she did regularly, hating uniformity. Which accounted for the fact that she was a bluehead this week, and was using cerulean lipstick whereas last week her hair and lips had blazed emerald green. Underneath the cosmetic customs of the day, she was a blonde—not a ravishing blonde, but you'd call her attractively pert and petite, with built-in cuteness.

Right now, she wanted the furniture in a double aisle effect, which she hoped Charley wouldn't mind. But then, he never objected to anything she did. He was meek and mild, always. And sweet. She loved him. Why? Because she loved him.

She tugged at the heavy 55-inch TV-console in the corner, hardly able to budge it.

"Allow me, madam," said a strong voice behind her.

She whirled, startled. "Charley! I didn't hear you come in, and you're home early; anything wrong, honey?"

"Nothing is wrong," said Becker, lifting the console off the floor, holding it suspended.

"Charley, your back," she cried in horror; "you'll sprain it. Let it down."

"Where does madam wish it placed?" Becker still held it as if it weighed a pound, instead of a hundred plus.

"Over there, against the violet wall. But, honey, you can't carry it way over there—"

She stopped and watched, her lips open. Becker was already across the room and swung it easily into position. He turned without panting.

Lora blinked her rosy lashes, in fascination.

"Charley, it's...well, before you used to puff and groan over lifting one small chair. Where in the world did you get all this he-man strength? Honest, I'm floored, honey. Well, say something, Charley. Don't just stand there."

"Do not call me Charley," said Charley Becker. "Nor other human endearments. They are out of place, madam; my factory designation is X-88."

After a blank moment, Lora twinkled happily.

"You got a raise, dear. That must be it. And they let you off early to tell me and celebrate. No wonder you're in such a good humor, playing jokes. Come and kiss me now, my great big he-man hero."

Becker ignored her arm-spread invitation. "Robots never become familiar with their masters or mistresses, in the human sense," he said in flat tones.

"A robot, eh?" teased Lora, rushing and hugging him. "Come on, squeeze me. Crush my ribs in your mighty steel embrace, tall, silver, and handsomely polished."

Becker let his arms hang, not responding. "That is exactly what would happen, madam; I would crush your ribs. What are your orders now? X-88 is your servant."

Lora laughed till the tears rolled.

"Honest, Charley, I never knew you had a sense of humor like that. It must have been a whopping raise and some big promotion. Won't tell yet? All right, have your fun. Meantime, what would you like for supper? Anything you want. What's your mouth watering for?"

"Oil," said Becker. "Grade 20, robo-refined, of atomic radiation 60 roentgens. It is the standard fuel for robots."

"Oil it is," said Lora gravely. "Lemon flavor? Or chilled, with whipped cream on top?"

Chuckling, she whirled to the kitchen, and rummaged in the Dinner Freeze for one of his favorites.

When they sat down at the table, five minutes later, Lora pointed at the bowl. "Your oil, X-88."

Becker raised it to his lips and took a swallow. He spat it out violently, but without emotion. "That is not oil, madam. That is jellied consommé."

Lora stared in dismay at the spattered smears on the wall. A trace of annoyance came into her voice. "Dear, isn't that carrying it a little, too far? It's your favorite, it always has been, and I thought you'd be pleased."

"Any human food products, taken internally, can cause a short circuit and severe damage, madam. Now my neck joint is stiff from that organic matter; it must be oiled."

Lora sighed, and decided to smile it all the way through, as her husband stalked to the tool closet, took out a can of oil, and squirted it around his neck, swiveling his head back and forth.

But Lora lost her smile when Charley unscrewed the top, tilted the can, and poured the rest down his throat.

Lora screamed.

LORA SAID, her face heavily overlaid with rose powder to hide the sleepless lines, "Yes, Doctor; my husband thinks he's a robot. He refused to come into bed last night. He just stood in the corner, like robots do for the night. Unmoving. All night." She continued after a moment. "In the morning he still stood there. He hadn't moved a muscle. Doctor, I—"

"Easy, Mrs. Becker," soothed the psychiatrist.

Dr. John Grady wore the pleasant face, quieting smile, and firm assurance of his profession. He was tidy in dress, relaxed in manner; he was objective and unemotional. He was sharp and penetrative in thought, able to leap like a bloodhound through the mazes of the human mind. His cases were all clinically interesting, but one must never pity the patient or his loved ones. Theoretically.

But Grady pitied Lora Becker. Theory be damned; she had a problem—a real stinker of a problem.

He turned professional again. "Your husband worked in a robot assembly factory? How long?"

"Nine years; he was in charge of tuning up their speech units."

"His job required him to speak to them and get their answers? Teach them? Train them to understand human language?"

Lora nodded. "He often told me how queer it was, even

142

though he did it a thousand times. How queer to suddenly find a machine talking back to you, with an almost human mind. He got to calling them 'he' and 'him' instead of 'it.'"

Dr. Grady studied that.

"Slow progression of personality projection. Giving them human status, in his mind. But still, harmless unless—tell me, Mrs. Becker. Did he ever worry about it? That is, did it bother him in some specific way, dealing with these humanlike mechanical men?"

Lora thought. "Yes, now that you mention it. I'd always kid him out of it, but sometimes he'd come home all nervous, telling me he had just murdered a robot."

"Murdered?"

"Well, some turned out defective; their mental units did not respond the right way. Charley called them 'idiots.' Or robot 'morons.' And useless then, of course. So he had to send an electric spark through the brain unit, burning it out. Whenever he did that, he'd sleep badly that night, just as if he had killed a man."

The psychiatrist processed that through his mental mill for a silent minute. "Anxiety neurosis," he said, tentatively. "Leading to retreat into robot identity himself. It was the only way, perhaps, that he could absolve himself of those 'killings.' The one way to ease his guilt complex. Charles Becker 'murdered' them; but not X-88, the robot. That freed him of guilt."

That was for her benefit, the simplification; they always felt better, hearing it put into clear-cut terms. They never understood the real diagnosis, bent and fractured emotions piled high like a pyramid, up which the investigator had to climb step by step, hoping to reach the apex.

There was the obvious fact that Becker was a puny man. No doubt all his adult life he had had to fend off the barbs. Hey, shorty. Every inch a mouse, ha-ha. My *dear*, no other woman would look at him once. No thanks, said the cannibal, I just had shrimp for breakfast.

Oh, it was understandable enough.

Yearnings created. Unfulfilled wish dreams. To be a big strong man. Or stronger than any man. Like a robot.

Also, as routinely recorded first by the nurse, they had no children—with his sterility at fault, not hers, as medically checked. Lack of male virility; again a steady hammering at his shrinking ego, day upon day.

Lora Becker was a good wife, no doubt of it. Loved him in spite of all. But in unguarded moments, little slips must have leaked past her lips. Oh, poor darling, don't strain yourself…that awful pawing Ed Ashley, big and strong sure but I'll take my little sweet boy anytime…really, dear, lots of men can't be fathers and the world is so full of brats already.

And then the robots, where he worked, giving human-like groans as they "died" under his hands. Weakness and unmanliness and robot brains stamped out. Guilt piled on guilt; the pyramid growing till it crushed him, cruelly.

All Becker's problems were solved in one stroke. Robots were not weaklings; robots never had children; and robots were at last rid of that human killer, Charles Becker.

That was his escape, free at last from all torment. That was the tangle to unravel, in its broad outline. Dr. Grady cut off his mental sketching. He had to be ready for the question they always asked. Always.

LORA WAS asking it, twisting her hands. "How serious is it, Doctor? Can he be—?"

So often they left the word out.

"Cured?" furnished Grady, softly, carefully. How many years had it taken him to eliminate all betraying inflections? "Now don't worry, Mrs. Becker; we acknowledge few hopeless cases here in 1972. Wait in the outer office, please, while I talk to him."

After Lora sat down in the waiting room and pretended to read a magazine with blurred eyes, Dr. Grady called to the small man standing like a statue in the corner, unobtrusively. But with the self-effacement of a trained robot, not of a meek man.

"This way please, Mr. Becker."

Becker did not turn his head, or even blink.

Grady nodded to himself. "This way please, X-88."

Becker came to life and obediently followed him into the private office. The door shut soundlessly.

"Lie on that couch," the doctor waved. "This will take an hour."

"I'll stand, sir; robots do not tire."

Grady allowed no trace of surprise or annoyance on his face, fixed in neutral pleasantness from long practice. "Yes, of course. As you choose. Your name?"

"X-88, sir. Robot home servant out of the Winton Works."

"The name Charles Becker. What does it mean to you?"

"Nothing, sir. However, the name Becker itself does; I am the robot servant of Mrs. Lora Becker."

"Ah, but if Lora Becker is married, she must have a husband. Where is he?"

"I do not know, sir."

"Is Mrs. Becker widowed or divorced?"

"No. That is, I don't know."

"Yes, you do know," said Grady, but not sharply. He said it casually, genially. "You answered correctly at first, before changing it. This shows that somehow, you yourself are fully aware that Mrs. Becker has a living husband, from whom she is not separated. Is he away on a trip?"

"No."

"Again you know the answer. Then where is he? It is an

interesting question, isn't it? Why would not her devoted husband show up all last evening and through the night?"

"Because he—I—" Becker stopped, turning blank. "A robot is unaware of human relationships and doings; I cannot answer."

"Yes, you can answer," said the psychiatrist patiently. His tone was unaccusing, friendly, persuasive. "You almost gave me the answer a moment ago. You are not a robot called X-88, are you? Think once; you are a man, a human being of flesh and blood, called Charles Becker. Isn't that right?"

Logic should bring him back, now.

Grady waited, hopefully. Had he broken through? Surely the preposterous fixation could not stand up in the face of pure logic. The robot masquerade must have weak chinks in its armor.

But the hard, set face did not change. "I am robot X-88," Becker said, in a nasal voice that exactly imitated the hundreds of robots he had activated into speech for nine years.

Dr. Grady sighed inwardly, conceding defeat for the time being. He had at least expected Becker to emerge a moment or two, bewildered, before retreating again into his robot fantasy. It was comparatively rare for such an utter change of personality to stick like glue this long, in its primary stages.

GRADY PICKED up a book on his desk, casually. Toying with it, he rose and approached the man who thought he was a robot. "Robots feel no pain, of course," he said.

"That is right, sir; robots feel no pain."

Grady suddenly jabbed the book at Becker, using its corners to dig into his ribs. Grady was not gentle about it, and he was a strong man.

Reaction, zero.

"As you said, sir, robots feel no pain."

Grady turned away. There must be a purple bruise there, under his clothes. No man could take sudden pain without at least a gasp; Becker hadn't flinched in the slightest.

The doctor's trained thoughts followed up the pattern. Complete transference of personality. Complete belief that he was a robot, an iron man, with an iron skin holding no pain nerves. Fakirs walking through live coals, or lying on beds of sharp nails. Ordinary people too, under fear and stress, carrying bad wounds without feeling them till later. Psychosomatic nerve block. It was of that near-incredible mental astigmatism to physical hurt.

Becker not only thought himself a robot. He *was* a robot. In all ways.

In all ways?

"A robot has three times the strength of a big man," stated Dr. Grady. "A robot could, for instance, raise one corner of my safe, there. Go and do it, X-88."

Becker stalked over without a word. He even imitated the slow, heavy tread of a three-hundred pound robot to perfection, with his soaking-wet 125; it was oddly humorous, in a quite humorless way.

Grady held his breath as Becker stooped for a handhold underneath the steel safe, standing on short legs. The human robot strained and lifted one corner off the floor, with his pipestem arms and frail back. Three powerful men could hardly have done the same.

Becker let it back silently, without a thump, as a well-trained, high-powered robot would. He turned and straightened, without triumph. Robots did not gloat.

"Very good," said Grady evenly. "As a robot, you could also jump out my window, fall ten floors, and land without harm, taking up the shock by trigger reflexes of your knee joints."

"That is right, sir."

Grady's eyes narrowed just a bit. The fear of death; the will to live—a man's strongest instinctive drive. Would Becker break down under that threat, and emerge from hiding in the shell of X-88?

"Go and jump out the window, X-88," said Grady, in direct order. Surely that would call his "bluff."

"Which window?" asked Becker, turning and walking toward the three that overlooked the street.

"The middle one," said Grady.

Becker was already halfway there, his step firm. He covered the rest of the distance, raised the window.

"Order rescinded," said Grady. "I have decided the jump is hardly necessary." Grady kept smiling; he had a hard-worn smile that could cover any inward shudder. "Return home now, X-88, with Mrs. Becker. Obey her implicitly in all things."

Dr. Grady toned up his smile for Lora as he patted her arm. "It went well but it will take time," he said softly. "Meanwhile, treat him as if he were your robot servant. Avoid calling him Charles or any endearment. Call him X-88. Give him household tasks to do, but nothing more. This is to erase all antagonism and resistance in him. Bring him back tomorrow."

Back in his office, before the next patient came in, Dr. Grady cast aside his smile. It was a unique case, the first he had heard of in psychiatric records, since robots had only been on the market for some twelve years. One thing struck him forcefully.

It would take time, he had told Lora Becker. It was one of the fundamental tenets of psychiatry to never hurry. To take your time. Never force things. There was no time limit in curing mental aberrations. No deadline to meet.

But with Charles Becker, there was a deadline.

Robots did not eat or drink human foods.

DR. GRADY was ready the next day. He had cancelled all his morning patients. They could wait; they ate and lived. He had concentrated all his thoughts on the new problem, and had his campaign worked out.

It had to break through fast. Fast. Charles Becker had been without food and drink for 48 hours already.

Grady wore his pleasant smile as Becker strode in, thumping his feet on the floor in slow measured steps.

"Charles Becker," said Grady, "is a killer of robots. At the factory from which you came, X-88, he was a worker. He often murdered defective robots; is that right?"

Becker's eyes flicked. "Yes, that is right."

Grady was pleased. X-88 now admitted knowing Charles Becker, where before he had denied it. A slight opening.

Grady wormed further in. "But robots do not have human status. Under the law, they are nothing but clever machines. Is a man, a human being, a murderer if he smashes a car, or a television set, or an electronic brain unit?"

"No," said Becker.

"A robot," said Grady, "is no more than a finer and more ingenious combination of the mechanical locomotion of a car, the perception of a sensitive TV-unit, and a compact electron brain. Therefore, Charles Becker was not committing murder when he destroyed robots; he only got rid of useless machinery. He would be foolish to have any sort of guilt complex over it, would he not?"

"I do not understand such human emotions."

Grady thought. *Defense mechanism.* As a robot, Becker did not need to follow the reasoning. Still intact. A mental barrier it was hopeless to attack. It was the root and foundation of his complex, built up solidly through nine long years.

Grady shifted the attack to concrete things. "Do you feel

weak, X-88?"

"No."

"But you've had no food for two days."

"Robots do not eat human food. However, four ounces of fuel must be given a robot each day, to keep him at peak performance; Mrs. Becker did not give me any."

No, thought Grady, *because I phoned her and said not to.* He had pressed the desk button and his nurse came in, wheeling a tea table loaded with hot steaming foods, directly before Becker. His nose could not fail to drink in the tempting aromas. His human stomach could not fail to hunger for what lay within reach.

Becker did not turn or move for five silent minutes. Grady gave up waiting. "Eat," he commanded.

"Sorry, but I must refuse," said Becker. "Human food is harmful to us; robots have built-in guards against obeying any commands harmful to them."

Grady smiled. Damnable. By the same token, he could not get any knockout drug down Becker's throat, to render him unconscious, and then force-feed him. Nor could ten men help him overpower Becker by sheer weight of numbers, for force-feeding. Becker would clamp his jaws shut, defying their fingers to open them; even if they managed to stuff food down his throat, he would automatically spit it out.

Force-feeding was out. Feeding of any kind was out until X-88 gave up the ghost and left.

The doctor signaled and the nurse wheeled the table out. He crossed that off his list on the desk. Then he brought a can of fuel-oil to Becker. It was ordinary oil, but looked quite like the poisonous radiated robot fuel. But it had another secret ingredient in it. Ipecac.

"Your fuel, X-88."

Becker drank it down. Robots drank their fuel like humans, down a fuel-pipe gullet to the fuel distribution system below. It was as mechanically efficient as any other way.

Becker stood a while, then retched violently over the rug.

As the nurse cleaned it up, Grady waited for Becker to explain it. If he was still a robot.

BECKER WAS still a robot. "That oil fuel was contaminated, sir; unfit for robot motors. But all late models are fitted with selective ejectors halfway to the fuel distributor system. Any unsuitable fuel is automatically regurgitated."

"Of course," smiled Grady. "Stupid of me to forget."

He drew a line through item two and shifted to item three.

"Punch a hole in this sheet metal with your fist," he said, pointing to a square-yard of steel 1/32 inch thick, held firmly in a stand and clamps.

Robots could smash a fist through gauges up to 1/32 inch; beyond that, they would shatter their intricate knuckle mechanisms.

Something had to work, Grady told himself. Something had to be insurmountable to the human limitations of Becker. Then he would begin to shed his fixation of X-88 the robot.

Hard steel, impervious to the human fist.

There was a loud noise as Becker's fist smashed through the steel plate. He withdrew the hand, without wincing. Knuckles unbruised, Grady noted. No blood. No broken bones sticking out under torn flesh.

Grady's pencil scraped across that item. Roughly, it was the well-known "maniacal" strength. Iron will, especially if psychotic, giving iron hardness momentarily to human bones and flesh. Hardly supernatural—merely the realm where supreme mental effort commanded all glandular and muscular processes to one powerful acme.

Mind over matter. A trite simplification but the nutshell of it, basically. Dr. Jekyll and Mr. Hyde. Charles Becker and

X-88.

Grady swung his thoughts to the next item.

BUT SUDDENLY, Lora came running in. Wild-eyed, she darted glances from the doctor to Becker, as if sensing failure. "I can't stand it any longer," she shrieked. Sobbing, she lifted the bottle to her lips. "Good-bye, dearest."

"Stop!" yelled Dr. Grady. "Don't drink that deadly poison." He stumbled over the rug clumsily, and was too late to stop her. She gulped the bottle down, swayed on her feet, fell. Grady caught her limp form.

"Your wife—dead," he said to Becker. "The woman you love."

"Charles Becker's wife," corrected X-88. "A robot does not love."

"Wait in the outer office again," said Grady, putting Lora on her feet. She cast a backward glance, choked, and closed the door behind her.

Grady crossed that off. Emotion, love. X-88 would have none of it.

"Strip yourself," ordered Grady. "Of all clothing."

Becker obeyed. It was no surprise to X-88 that he wore human clothing. Most robot servants did in human homes, to hide their metallic shine and make them less alien. Most people wanted it that way.

Becker stood nude.

"Robots are sexless," stated Grady.

"Yes."

"But humans have sex organs," said the doctor simply, holding a large mirror in the right position. "How can X-88 have the same?"

"I have no sex organ, sir; I am a robot."

Grady tilted the mirror. "Your face. What do you see?"

"I see shiny metal reflected," said Becker. "The usual TV

eye-units, false nose, mouth for fuel intake. No human beard or hair."

Grady put the mirror away. Complete visual illusion. Looking at his own body, Becker's eyes refused to see what could not exist on a robot. Sex organ, head of hair, fingernails, navel—none of those existed for X-88.

But Grady did not tell Becker to dress. He still stood nude. The emotion of love he had denied. There was a stronger instinctive drive; he buzzed twice in signal.

Lora came in, not the nurse. She stared at her unclothed husband without surprise.

"Ready to go through with it?" the doctor asked gently.

Lora blushed but nodded.

"I'm glad you agreed," said Grady. "If you hadn't, I'm afraid I would have been forced to insist. I'll leave the room. Take all the time you need. There is a closet for your clothes. When you wish me back, press the desk button." He touched her hand. "Remember, try your best. It's important. And it can't wait for another time and place."

Lora watched the door close on the doctor. Then, glancing at the nude figure of her husband with another blush, she began undressing. She stood before him all the while, deliberately. His eyes did not focus on her at all. Did not seem to see the soft white thighs revealed, the womanly curves.

Lora blushed no more. It was like undressing in complete personal privacy among inanimate furniture. But she went on desperately and finally stood before him, dropping the last bit of clothing coyly. Charles Becker had always responded to her charms—always.

WHEN DR. GRADY answered the buzzer and strode in, Lora shook her head in anguish, fixing the last button. "He ignored me. Like a—a robot."

She fled to the waiting room, leaving a trail of tears.

Grady drew a line again on his list. The sex drive was completely absent in robots, including X-88.

He had already checked with Lora on other bodily functions, and knew it was a blind alley. Robots did not eliminate waste products; neither did X-88. But that was comparatively simple—cessation of digestion, and metabolism slowed down to the minimum required for mere basic existence. Intestines, kidneys, all internal organs under rigid control.

One more item left.

But this was the clincher, and Grady had expected it to come down to this finally; at least, the proceeding had perhaps opened the way. Placed some tiny doubt in the mind of X-88. Enough to burst the floodgates over one final inconsistency in his hallucination.

Then X-88 would leave. Charles Becker would return, and in time for a hearty meal before he collapsed from hunger. Lack of food had no meaning to X-88, but could be carried to an extreme of slow starvation for submerged Becker.

This final item had to get Becker out of his iron trap, thought Grady, and the play of words did not amuse him.

Grady opened his desk drawer, but first, in preparation, he said, "Remember this, X-88. Charles Becker, who worked at the robot assembly plant, is not a killer. Not a murderer. No guilt hangs over him. For nine years, only doing his job and burning out the brain-units of defective robots, he let that false thought loom in his mind. Without reason. He is innocent. He can return and face the world without stigma or disgrace. Charles Becker, wherever he is hiding now, has no slightest reason not to return. Is that clear?"

"I understand nothing of what you say," said the man robot.

No, thought Grady, *but your ears heard the words and your mind recorded them. Your human mind. You will remember.*

Grady stepped forward. He had a sharp knife in his hand. "Robots do not bleed," he said. "They have no blood; you have no blood. Is that right, X-88?"

"I have no blood," agreed Becker, unflinching.

"I will plunge this knife into you. There will be no blood, of course."

"No blood."

That was established. The stage was ready. Blood dripping. X-88 would see it, feel it, unable to explain it away. Unable to explain his soft vulnerability. X-88 would leave; Charles Becker would come back, bleeding.

It had greater significance, too. Something which allowed Grady to pin his confidence on it strongly. Man was born of woman, in blood. In that flow of blood, Charles Becker would be born again. A strong fundamental memory association, vibrating in every fiber of every man since life began.

Grady slowly raised the knife. He poised for a moment. He plunged the knife at Becker, who stood stolid, waiting. It must be a deep wound, short of fatal, letting blood gush. An artery. No half measures; easy enough to doctor him for that later.

Grady used the full power of his muscular arm. Grady pulled back the knife after the third hard thrust at three different parts of the body. Grady stared at the knife.

Grady slowly walked to his desk. He crossed off the last item. He dropped the pencil. He thought ahead to the report he would make to the psychiatric people, jolting them. Jolting all their pleasant smiles from their calm faces.

How skin and flesh could turn to iron. Biologic iron, as strong as steel. Stronger than steel. He dropped the knife with its dulled point and twisted blade. Shiny. Unbloody. Intravenous injection of food? The last road was blocked.

Dr. Grady held onto his smile, for Lora. But he wondered how he could tell her.

Not that she would be a widow soon; that she had been a widow for three days already.

THE END

Subject to Change

By
RON GOULART

PENDLETON had been away from San Francisco over two months. The airport taxi left him at his place, where he showered and shaved. Then he decided he would walk, down through Chinatown and over into North Beach, to Beth's apartment.

It was a warm Saturday afternoon and he unbuttoned his Dacron blazer a block or so into Chinatown. He smiled as he wandered by the bright restaurants and shops, the rows of ivory Buddhas in window after window. On one corner Pendleton stopped and took a deep breath, watching a scattering of tourists taking pictures of each other. Someone had lost a half dozen fortune cookies on the sidewalk and they crackled and spread fragments and fortunes as people passed.

While he was waiting for a signal to change, three small Chinese boys charged a fourth who had ducked around Pendleton. They all ran around the corner and Pendleton looked after them. There was an old curio and toyshop there. He went toward its streaked window, trying to identify the objects. Some kind of procession of tin soldiers made up the main display. The door of the shop opened and an old man with a flared white beard came out. His dark suit hung loose on him and his tie was coming untied as he hurried away.

The old man brushed by Pendleton, nudging him. "Many pardons," he said, cutting across the street. He ran downhill, weaving a little, and into an alley.

The bells over the toy shop door rattled again. "Stop, thief!" shouted the fat Chinese, who came running up to

Pendleton. The man shouted again and stopped on the corner, his hands on his hips, looking.

Pendleton crossed the street and turned down the alley the old man had used. This would cut off a block of the way to Beth's. He had kept quiet about the thief because he didn't want to get involved in a lot of delaying questioning.

HALFWAY down the alley he saw an arm dangling out of a garbage can. Pendleton blinked and approached the shadowed area around the can. He flipped the lid up and the coat sleeve that had been tangled on the can edge slipped free and dropped into the can. If the old man was wandering around naked, they shouldn't have much trouble catching him.

Pendleton liked the pre-quake apartment house Beth lived in. In almost any weather he liked to see its narrow brown wood front waiting there in the middle of the block. He smiled as a big blue-gray gull flew low overhead and then circled up and away behind Beth's building. Pendleton took the rough steps in twos and threes and swung at Beth's bell. There was a folded note for him glued on her mail box lid with Scotch tape. It told him she might be delayed a bit and to get her keys from under the rubber-plant pot on the porch and let himself in. He did that, thinking again that Beth's notes always looked as though she wrote them on horseback.

Upstairs he dropped her keys on the small mantle over the small real fireplace. Her bedroom door was slightly open. Just as he noticed this, Beth called out to him.

"I hope that's you, Ben?" she said from her room.

"Where'll I put the ice, lady?" he said. "You're supposed to be out."

"Welcome back. I just got here and I had to change so I left the keys down there in case you got here while I was changing. How was New York?"

"Okay, but I'm glad I'm with the agency out here. How'd you get in without keys?" He sat down in the soft tan sofa chair he'd given her.

"I have a key to the kitchen way. Is the show all right now?"

"I guess we fixed it for a while. How are you?"

"Fine. And, hey, I have a good part in Alex's new play. It just happened and I couldn't write."

"You have lousy handwriting, you know," Pendleton called. Grinning, he got out a cigarette and reached into his coat pocket for a book of matches. Something jabbed into the palm of his hand.

"It's because I'm so intense," Beth said, near her bedroom door.

Pendleton winced and pulled a small toy Chinese junk out of the pocket. The price stamp was still on the bottom of the boat, 25 cents. The old man must have dropped it in his pocket when he nudged him.

Beth came up behind him. "It's warm in here. Give me your coat. I have a whole new concept about making martinis. This fellow in Actors' Lab told me. You do it with Zen." Her hands rested on Pendleton's shoulders.

"I'll be damned," he said, rubbing his palm with the boat as he stood.

Beth slid her arms over his shoulders and locked her hands on his chest. "What's that, Ben?"

Pendleton turned around in her hold. He tapped her tanned nose with the toy boat and told her about it. "I suppose I should take it back," he said finally.

Beth laughed. "Makes you a receiver of stolen goods." She took the toy boat and walked to the fireplace. She put it next to her keys and turned to him. She was wearing a light blue dress with a flared skirt. No stockings, flat black shoes. She'd cut her blonde hair short since he'd seen her last.

"Welcome back," she said, smiling.

A light wind was starting up, tapping windows with tree branches, as Pendleton let himself into Beth's darkening apartment. He flipped the light switch on and started for the tan sofa chair, jiggling the keys in his hand. The bedroom door slammed.

"You in there?" Pendleton called. Her note said she'd gone out for some forgotten groceries.

Pendleton opened the bedroom door and turned on the lights. The window beyond Beth's low, blue-covered bed was open and the wind was flapping the curtains against her dressing table. A strong flap caught a lipstick and flipped it into the thick rug.

Edging around the bed, Pendleton closed the window and picked up the lipstick. He left the bedroom door a bit open and went back to the chair. There was a paper back by Eisenstein on the coffee table and he picked that up and read down the contents page.

The wind got stronger and parts of the old building creaked, first something down under him, then something way up and to the right. Now and then there would be a bang from out in back. Pendleton dropped the book and got down on his knees in front of the fireplace and kindled a fire. As the fire took hold, bright sparks popped out into the room.

Something started tapping on the window behind Pendleton's chair. At last, in a lull between creaking and banging, he became aware of the tapping. He looked at the window and the early night sky. The tapping went on.

There was a gray cat sitting on the sill outside. The cat was tangled up in an orange and blue bead necklace. "Lonely out there," Pendleton said. He didn't much like cats, but this one looked sad. He opened the window and the cat jumped in, the necklace falling free and clattering against the wall. "We'll see if maybe Beth's got something around to give to wandering cats." Pendleton reached out to pick up the cat. Sputtering, the animal raked at his fingers and dived between his legs.

Pendleton spun and saw the cat scoot through the open bedroom door. "Hey, you little bastard, you'll knock over things."

He was two steps from the door when it slammed and locked. Pendleton stopped, wondering how the animal had managed to bang into the door hard enough to close it. He didn't think the cat should stay in there and anyway Beth would want to get in when she got home. He'd pick the lock. Crouching, he reached for the knob. Something clicked and the door swung in. He recognized Beth's terry robe and he looked up and saw her face, very pale.

"Okay," she said. "I guess I was too cute with the key bits. Go away, Ben, and leave me alone. Please?"

"What's the matter?" He was still squatting and her stepping forward sent him over.

"Just go away, Ben. Please, now." She brushed by him and sat in a bucket chair, putting both bare feet down hard on the floor.

Ben got himself up. "You drunk?"

BETH brushed at her hair. "I thought if you were sitting out here and I showed up in the bedroom, you'd think I came in the back way. Or that I was already in there and just hadn't heard you." She bit her thumb. "Just another trick I wanted to try."

"What are you talking about?" He bent and scooped up the bead necklace.

"Go away. That's all."

"Well, why?" He twisted the string of beads around his

161

knuckles. "Somebody else?"

"Yes. Alex." She smiled.

"Alex? That fruiter who runs the Actors' Lab." The string broke and beads splattered away from him. Three landed in the fire.

"Or maybe my Uncle Russ. Did you know we lived with him for three years when I was a kid and I was always having odd fevers and things? He had some kind of quack x-ray business."

Pendleton took Beth's shoulders. "You're sick, is that it?"

"No. Go away, Ben."

"Well, what is it?"

Beth sighed, annoyed. "You know about Method. You have to feel the parts, live them."

"Sure."

Beth shrugged her shoulders until Pendleton let go. "One weekend afternoon—oh, about two or three weeks after the agency sent you off—I was here trying to be an old lady. For an exercise at the Lab. And I was."

Pendleton blinked at her still pale fact. "That's swell, Beth. A guy likes to know what his fiancée is up to while he's away."

"I *was* an old lady." She stood with her body thrust almost against him. "See? I changed."

He backed a little. "How about a drink?"

"Don't you get it, Ben? How the hell do you think I just came in?"

"The back way." Pendleton decided to try a drink on her and then find out who her doctor was these days.

"I was the cat. Now you know about it and can go away, Ben." She let herself fall to the floor and she huddled there, crying.

"How long have you had this idea?" He knelt beside her, running one hand over her back.

"You know who put that silly damn boat in your pocket?" she asked.

"Sure. You were that little old man."

Beth rolled and sat up, her legs tangled in the robe. She took a deep breath. "Listen, Ben. I got a kick out of changing into different kinds of people. It was a help in my work at the Actors' Lab. Then I got the idea it would be fun to try other things. Animals, chairs, tables. One rainy night I was a footstool until it was time to go to bed."

"I was a tea kettle as a boy. Stop kidding."

"I don't know, Ben. It gets sort of vacant all around when you're away somewhere. I had this feeling that I wanted to see if I could just step into a store or someplace and try to swipe something. Anything."

PENDLETON found himself starting to shake. He put his arms around Beth. "That was you, then, taking junk from an old Chinese."

"I could change, you see, and take things as all sorts of odd characters. If I was spotted and followed, I'd try to duck in an alley or a doorway and change again. The clothes are extra. Sometimes I could hide clothes in a lot. Most of the time, though, I'd have to change into something new. A bird, a cat. Then I'd carry what I had stolen in my beak or around my neck." She laughed softly. "Once I copped an umbrella and changed into a big dog and went off with it in my mouth." She twisted slightly in his arms. "I'm sorry. It's all sort of odd and silly. I do it."

"Well, why?"

"I don't know."

"Beth?" He inched up, lifting her with him.

"Yes?" She let him sit her in the sofa chair.

"You have to go see somebody. You have to stop."

She stiffened. "If it was as simple as insanity, I would."

"Please, Beth." He wandered to the fireplace and threw in more wood.

"The stealing *does* bother me. I think the changing is good. I can use it to really go someplace in my acting career. Quit the secretary business altogether. I actually changed to an old woman for one of Alex's one-acters. He thought I'd just done a good job of makeup. I don't believe I want to simply stop, Ben."

"You have to!"

"Don't start shouting commands."

Pendleton sat across from her on the sofa. "Will you promise to start seeing somebody? Maybe I can find out about a good man. Promise you'll see him…"

"You going to ask around? Why don't you do a TV spot? 'We are happy to announce that Beth Gershwin is daffy.'"

"Relax, Beth. You decide what you want to do. I won't talk to anybody."

Beth moved to the window. The wind had died. "I don't know, Ben."

"Let it rest. Let's have that drink." He came to her side.

"I think I'd like to be alone for a while."

"I'd like to stay."

"I'd like you to go. Please."

"Beth."

"Go on, Ben." She stared at him, then walked into her bedroom.

She didn't close the door and he followed.

Her robe was spread-eagled on the bed. Pendleton looked around the room. Before, there had been one carved stool at the vanity table. Now there were two.

Pendleton left the apartment and ran down the hall, taking short, shallow breaths. But he couldn't just leave her. He bit his lip and went back through the still open door.

"Come on, Beth. Don't be stubborn," he said into the

bedroom, watching the two stools.

He waited an hour. Then he turned off the lights and started to leave. Going out this time, he stepped on one of the wooden beads and almost fell onto the coffee table.

Pendleton slammed Beth's door and went out into the clear night. If she could be stubborn, so could he.

IT WAS almost two weeks before she called him to apologize. She'd got him at the agency. He didn't stay in his apartment much. He kept talking to himself if he did.

You could see the street from the little Italian restaurant they'd agreed to meet in. Pendleton sat at a round table close to the wide window and watched for Beth. There was a slight haze in the afternoon air and most of the secretaries that passed were coatless.

Beth started smiling a quarter of a block from him. She was in a light cotton dress, weaving in and out of the noontime pedestrians.

"Nice day," Pendleton said, standing.

Beth smiled and sat down. "I noticed that right off."

They ordered and Pendleton said, "How've you been?"

"Great." She clasped her hands together on the checkered tabletop. "You were right, Ben. I'm sorry I was mean."

Pendleton moved his glass of water three inches. "Good."

"I've started seeing a very highly recommended analyst. Things are starting to look up." I haven't even had an impulse to filch anything in days."

The food arrived. "It'll take time."

"I have a great part in Alex's next play. It's really a challenge. By Ionesco. Being able to change will help."

Pendleton set his fork down. "Huh?"

"I tried changing into the character last night. It came off fine."

"What are you seeing a psychiatrist for, then?" he asked,

his voice low.

"So I won't steal things any more."

He held the edge of the table for a minute, not meeting her eyes. Finally he said, "I see. Well, that's fine, Beth. How've things been at work?"

Beth grinned and told him.

THE DAYS were turning cool and the trees had started scattering dry leaves into the wind. On a sharp weekend afternoon Pendleton was killing time in the produce district before driving over to Beth's.

There was a coffee shop open and Pendleton thought about crossing over for a cup of coffee. The whitewashed door of the place shot open and a fat woman with an orange-fringed shawl came out. She was carrying something wrapped up in a paper napkin. She glanced at Pendleton, hesitated a second and then went running off toward a closed warehouse. By the time she reached it, the short-order cook was on the street looking after her. He threw a gesture after her and went back inside.

Pendleton shivered once slightly. He started walking for his car and a block from it he found himself running. He got to Beth's place ahead of the approaching dusk.

The downstairs door wasn't locked, but Beth's apartment door didn't open when he tried it. Pendleton grunted, slapping his pockets for something to pick the lock with.

The door opened. Beth, in capris and a striped sweater, looked out at him, her head tilted slightly to one side. "Did I hear applause? You're early."

"You know why I'm here early." He pushed into the room. "I thought you were better. What the hell were you doing down there?"

"Where? What's the matter?" She backed across the rug to the fireplace. A small fire was going and she turned to warm her hands at it.

"I just saw you steal something from that diner. Silverware maybe. You want me to search the place?"

Facing him, her lips hardly parted, Beth said, "I should think you would trust me, being we love each other and all. I was rehearsing until a half-hour ago and Alex dropped me off. I've been here since then."

Pendleton's hands fell to his sides. "Well, nothing I guess is wrong. I'm just jumpy. This changing thing bothers me."

Beth reached out and patted his arm. "It's okay. Ben?"

"Yeah." He sat down in the tan chair and looked up at her.

"Want to eat here tonight, by the fire? I'll have the Flying Something deliver food."

"Good. And send out for a bottle or two."

Beth bent and kissed him. "Trust me again?"

He brushed at her hair and nodded.

PENDLETON dropped too much wood into the fireplace and a stick snapped out onto the rug. He gingerly picked up the stick and poked it back into the flames. He went back to the low sofa Beth was on. He found his glass in the dark and refilled it from the pitcher.

Beth reached out with one bare foot and stroked the side of his head. She had put on a dark blue dress with several stiff lace petticoats and whenever he tried to touch her she made crackling sounds.

"You're really a nice fellow," Beth said, finding his ear with her toe.

"So are you," he said, finishing his drink.

"Maybe we should go ahead and get married."

Ben agreed and poured fresh drinks.

"Ben?"

"Yeah?"

"I'm sorry." She was crying.

"What is it?"

"It *was* me this afternoon. I *have* been doing those things. I never went to any highly recommended man at all."

Pendleton felt tolerant. "So what? Things will work out somehow."

BETH sat up. "I can't stop it, Ben."

Pendleton thought he heard an odd quaver in her voice. "You're not onstage now, kid. Save the phony touches."

Her leg swung round, just missing his head, and she stood up. "That's your trouble. You're totally incapable of comprehending."

"I comprehend you. You're loony and a liar."

Beth slapped him. "It'll be simpler if I stop being me!"

Pendleton had somehow gotten his arm stuck under the sofa. "Take it easy."

He was aware of a rustling sound and when he got loose and came up he saw Beth naked by the window for an instant. As he looked she changed. Then there were two tan sofa chairs in the room.

Pendleton called Beth's name over and over, but she wouldn't come back. It got cold in the apartment after a time and he threw all the wood he could find in the fire. He crawled over to the martini pitcher and drank from it. He noticed that some sticks had fallen out and landed in the tangle of petticoats Beth had left and he smiled at the disorder of everything and put his head back against the sofa.

Petticoats crackling woke him. Even before he got his head up very high in the room, he was coughing. The room was turning bright, sparkling orange.

"Beth!" he said. "Beth!"

There were still the two tan sofa chairs.

"Beth, sober up now! Come on, change! We've got to get

168

out!"

Nothing happened. Pendleton looked at the chairs a moment. The one on the left. He grabbed it up and wavered to the apartment door. To make sure, he'd have to come up for the other one.

For several minutes it seemed the chair would stay wedged in the doorway. It came free finally and he went back with it and tumbled and twisted down the stairs.

A SIREN met him in the cold night outside. The engines were already there. The firemen were heading for the building.

Spray fell back across the street where Pendleton took the chair. "Beth, please," he said in a low voice. "Change now." He tried to go get the other chair, to be sure, but they wouldn't let him.

He fell into the one he'd picked and began crying softly. The sirens stopped. Before he let the ambulance people look at him, he insisted that the chair be looked after.

No trace of Beth was found and Pendleton couldn't explain what had happened. After they let him go, he had the chair sent to his apartment.

He put it very carefully in the living room by the liquor cabinet and sat down near it to wait.

THE END

The Show Must Go On

By
HENRY SLESAR

*Actors wanted: experience unnecessary, salary excellent,
life expectancy brief...*

HE AWOKE in darkness, trembling with the thought of escape.

His hands groped around the floor, trying its solidity. Then he crawled forward with agonizing slowness until his fingertips found a wall. He raised himself to his feet, his cheek scraping the cool surface of the enclosure.

An idea came to him, and he slapped at the pocket of his shirt. His palm struck the outline of something. Matches!

He lit one, and raised it to the level of his wide, frightened eyes. He was facing a door, a barricade of steel, without sign of latch or doorknob. But there was a sign, and he read it in the flicker of the match-flame. It said:

PUSH

He made a noise in his throat, and shoved against the door. It gave in to his weight, and he was outside the building, standing in a courtyard washed softly by moonlight.

He circled where he stood, and knew he was a prisoner still. A wire fence, four times his height, surrounded him.

He came closer to it, and plunged his fingers through the mesh, rattling it helplessly in his misery. Then he saw the second sign, and held his breath. It read:

YOU CAN DO IT

Encouraged, he began his climb. The toes of his rubber-soled shoes fit neatly into the openings, and he gained the summit of the fence quickly. He swayed uncertainly at the top, and almost dropped the twenty-five feet to the other side. But he regained his balance, clambered down the mesh, and dropped panting to the ground.

A voice boomed at him.

"All right, let's go! We haven't got all night!"

He forced himself to his feet, and looked for the source of the sound with wild movements of his head. He could see nothing but the menacing shadows of a crowded forest. With a frightened glance over his shoulder, he plunged into the thick of it, hoping to find a pathway to the unknown freedom he sought.

He thrashed through the tangled vines for a small eternity, and then gave up with a sob. He fell against a tree trunk, dampening the bark with his tears.

This time, the voice was quieter, but its tone was impatient.

"Keep going, keep going! To the right. The right!"

He clung to the tree as if for protection, and then, with a gasp, plunged once more into the darkness.

He found the clearing, to the right.

It was like an arena, with spectator trees, and with bright eyes winking at him through the leaves.

There was a log to the left of the cleared green circle, and a frail young girl in torn clothing sat on it, huddled with either fear or cold. She was clutching something like an infant to her chest.

He came closer and saw that it was a broadsword. He paused.

"Who are you?" he said.

She looked up at him, her expression savage.

"You're here!" she said.

He took a step forward, and the voice spoke once more.

"Kill her and you go free."

171

"No!" he shouted.

"Kill him and go free," said the voice.

The girl put her head in her arms. Her shoulders shook.

He walked towards her and she screamed.

"No, please!" he said painfully. "I won't hurt you. Why should I hurt you?"

She looked at him narrowly. Her hand tightened around the handle of the sword. *"You* know why," she accused.

"You must trust me," he said. He put his hand out gently to her. She backed away from his touch, and leaped off the log. She moved away cautiously, gripping the weapon with both hands.

"Use the sword," said the voice. *"Strike, and go free."*

She trembled, and lifted the sword from the ground. The man whirled, eyes penetrating the forest for an escape route. He backed up, and fell over a trailing root.

"Now," said the voice. *"Strike!"*

The girl moved towards him hypnotically.

"I hate you...I hate you..." she moaned. She lifted the blade high, and the man lashed out with his foot as she towered over him. The broadsword flew from her grasp.

"Now kill her," said the voice. *"And you can go free."*

"I WON'T!" he shouted again. He scrambled to his feet and made a dive for the weapon. He took it in his hand and waved it threateningly at the surrounding woods.

"Come out! Come out!" he screamed. The eyes of the forest blinked back at him in silence.

He flung the sword from his hand, as if in loathing. Then he crashed into the forest once more.

THE PRODUCER gurgled through his hookahmatic. Frick, his assistant, recognized this symptom of official disgust, and jumped to his fed.

"Turn it off!" the Producer said, gesturing towards the fidelivision screen. Frick turned it off. "No, leave it on," the Producer moaned, peeping at the white oblong through his chubby fingers. "Let's see what Manford does in *this* pickle." Frick turned it on.

"He'll probably drop in the dinosaur film," he said.

"If he does, I get a new Director," the Producer answered in a rumbling voice. "He's used that spot three times in the past month."

The fidelivision flashed. A screaming red title dripped bloodily across the screen. "MAN AGAINST DINOSAUR!" it said. The Producer's angry cry almost drowned out the horrific roar of the live-prop brontosaurus that appeared.

"Meeting, meeting!" he cried. "We're going to have a staff meeting—right after the show!"

"A *live* meeting?" Frick gasped.

"A live one," the Producer said. "Everybody here—right here—in person! This is an emergency!"

"Gosh, T. D.—" Frick frowned disapprovingly. "That's kind of rough, isn't it? I mean, a phonescreen session would be a lot simpler. It'll take hours for Manford and the rest of 'em to get through the Jam."

"I don't care," the Producer said petulantly. "This kind of bumbling inefficiency has gone far enough. It'll do 'em good to get crushed in the Traffic for a change—"

Frick paled, obviously disturbed by the severity of the punishment the Producer was meting out. Only the lowest ranks of employees, the non-executives, the factory people, were forced to suffer the indignities of the Jam.

"I'm sure they'll get that fellow," Frick said. "After all, T. D.—how far can he get? When he gets out of the forest, he'll reach the Studio Barrier, and he'll be stopped. Simple as that."

"And what if he finds the exit?"

Frick scoffed. "Well, the odds on that—"

"Odds? Don't talk to me about odds, Frick!" The Producer winced as man and brontosaurus came together on the screen. There was a close-up of the man's face, and his expression wasn't pretty when he saw the imitation beast. But of course, he couldn't know it was harmless—

"The letters!" the Producer groaned. "The complaints! I can see 'em now—"

The office door opened. A pretty redhead with vacant eyes and a frozen smile poked her head inside.

"What is it, Miss Stitch?"

"Will you take a call from Mr. Manford? Phonescreen Seven."

"You bet I will," the Producer said menacingly.

Frick lowered the fidelivision sound and flicked on P. S. 7 with a few efficient motions. The face of Joe Manford, the Director of the night's *Thrill Show*, was haggard, despite the jovial smile.

"Hi, T. D.," he said. "Been watching the show?"

"Yes, Joseph," the Producer said gravely.

"Oh." The smile faded, but only for a moment. "Well, nothing to worry about. Our boys will have that fellow rounded up in a few minutes. Can't imagine how that got fouled up. But that's the *Thrill Show* for you. Full of surprises."

"Is that a fact?" said the Producer. He picked up the butt of his hookahmatic and sipped smoke calmly. "I presume this fellow was fully authorized before you put him on?"

"Oh, yes," Manford said hastily. "He passed the routine FCC physical, and had the usual adrenaline and hypnomecholyl dose. I mean, you saw the girl didn't you? She was *fine*, wasn't she?" He beamed.

"Yes," said the Producer. "She certainly was fine." Frick stirred uncomfortably behind him.

"Anyway," the Director continued, "we're dropping in the dinosaur film—that's always good for a few shivers—and we've sent a crew into the Studio to get that man out of there—"

The Producer nodded his head toward his assistant. "Frick," he said, eyes on Manford. "You tell him."

Frick stepped into range. He cleared his throat and looked at the floor. "There'll be a meeting after the show," he mumbled.

"Meeting?" Manford said. "What for?" He blinked, and looked at Frick's bowed head. Then he looked dazed. "You don't mean a—a *live* meeting?"

Frick nodded. The Producer puffed contentedly on his hookahmatic. He blew a smoke ring, and it puffed itself to pieces against the phonescreen.

THE MAN raised himself from the ground. His limbs felt weak, and he had to force the breaths through his lungs.

He got to his feet, feeling somewhat stronger. The forest seemed as impenetrable as ever, but he faced its challenge now with more confidence.

That girl! he thought. My God—she was really going to kill him! He shook his head bewilderedly. Such a young, pretty girl! What had he done to her? What made her want to do it?

He moved through the forest slowly, ducking branches, trailing the sources of dim lights in the distance. But as he approached, they proved to be illusory, odd reflections of moonlight among the trees.

She didn't *want* to kill him, not really. He could sense that. It was something more. She was *compelled* to do it—that was it. Someone had put her up to it. But who? Who hated him enough?

The speculation made his headache. He blanked out his

thoughts and decided to concentrate on his predicament. There had to be a way out. The girl had entered the forest at some point. But where?

He heard the sound of voices, and he stopped breathing.

"Manford means business," one of them said.

"He's plenty worried. T. D. was watching tonight—"

"The sponsors kick T. D., T. D. kicks Manford, and Manford kicks us. Who do we kick?"

"I don't know about you. I got an old dog home—"

"Okay. Let's separate and find this bird."

"Right. Hey, Lou! Let's have some tracer lights!"

He concealed himself in the brush as a burst of light exploded over the treetops. He watched the men parade past; ordinary-looking men, executive types, with white collars and knit ties and flannel suits. Strangely enough, they seemed quite at home in this wilderness.

He waited until they passed his hiding place. Then he started on a nimble run in the direction from which they had come.

THE PRODUCER fitted himself snugly into Executive position: desk, swivel chair, and man welded into one solid, efficient unit. He sighed a comfortable sigh, and glanced up at the wall clock. Ten-thirty. The *Thrill Show* would be over in half an hour; the dinosaur film would wind it up neatly. He'd probably have some explaining to do to the sponsors tomorrow, but he was all prepared to give the usual "popular demand" argument.

He regretted the live meeting he had called. It would be two hours at least before the Staff plowed through the Traffic Jam. That meant he couldn't leave the office until after one-thirty.

He looked at the hopeless tower of papers on his desk blotter. Most of them were letters, and his secretary had never quite gotten the hang of weeding out the chaff. Once he found a letter from an FCC Vice-President in the Discard File; since then, he ordered all mail to his desk. He wished he could get a better secretary than Miss Stitch, but the shortage of A1-rated secretaries (A for "Attractiveness," 1 for Efficiency) was acute.

He skimmed through the top of the pile quickly.

"Dear Mr. Donnelly... Certainly enjoyed 'Death in the Ring'...one of the best *Thrill Shows* I've ever seen...wonder if you would consider a football thriller I have in mind called 'Murder Kicks Off'..."

"Dear Mr. Donnelly... Let's have more shows like 'Snake Pit'...that Mother and Baby idea was the greatest...I really thought that woman would go nuts when she saw her kid with the cobra... A shocker all the way..."

"Dear Mr. Donnelly... If 'Kiss of Death' was your idea of entertainment, you ought to retire...that sort of sex schmaltz went out with television...give us real gutsy stuff and never mind the mush... I'm only eleven years old, but I'll bet I could write a better scenario than that... I have this idea for a show called..."

"Dear Mr. Donnelly..."

The Producer sighed again. He reached into his pill drawer and took an ulcer capsule. Then he went back to his correspondence.

When the man entered his office, he didn't even glance up.

"That you, Frick?" he said, eyes on a letter of praise from a Yonkers housewife.

When the man didn't answer, the Producer looked up.

He gasped. "Hey!" he said.

"Shut up!" the man said harshly. He moved swiftly to-wards the desk and lifted a bronze ashtray in a lightning motion. He raised the object threateningly over the fat man's head.

"Keep quiet!" he said.

"What is this?" The Producer's voice quavered. Then he recognized the face. "You're the one from the Show—"

The man blinked. His face relaxed, and he lowered the impromptu weapon. "I—I'm sorry…"

The Producer came around the side of the desk. He took the ashtray from his hand, and helped him into the interview chair. The man collapsed limply at his touch.

"How'd you get here?" the Producer said.

"I don't know," the man mumbled. "I found a door…back there…" He buried his chin on his chest. His clothes were shredded, and his hands were trembling.

"Take it easy," the Producer told him. He poked his finger on a desk button. The signal brought Frick into the office.

"What's up, T. D.?" Then the assistant saw the man in the chair. "My God," he whispered, swallowing hard. "Gosh, I'm terribly sorry, T. D.—"

"Never mind being sorry," the Producer said gratingly. "Let's just be thankful he found his way here instead of into the street. If he'd been picked up by the Police—"

The assistant mopped his brow. "That would have been terrible. They'd surely recognize him from the show. If the FCC saw him in this condition—"

"Yes," the Producer said grimly. "If they saw him in this condition, their medical office would slap an injunction on us so fast—we'd *all* be out in the Jam. Do you realize that?"

Frick blanched. "I'll get Dr. Stark in here right away. We'll get him an anti-dope shot immediately—"

"That girl…" the man said.

"It's okay, fella," Frick said. "You're okay now."

"Never mind him," said the Producer. "Get Spier in here. Right away!"

Frick hurried out. The Producer poured a slug of brandy into a cup and held it to the man's lips. He gulped it gratefully, and then exploded a rasping cough. When the cough subsided, he buried his head on his chest again, breathing heavily.

The Producer studied the man's face. It was oddly familiar.

"Say," he said. He put his hand under the chin and lifted the face up. The eyes opened. "Aren't you Jerry Spizer?"

The man stared blankly. The Producer grunted. "Huh. Guess you don't know *who* you are right now, fella. But you're Jerry Spizer, all right. Imagine that!" T. D. shook his head. "The great Spizer. In a *Thrill Show!*" He chuckled dryly.

The doctor bustled into the office, a small cyclone, trailing the nervous assistant behind him like a flurrying dust cloud.

"Roll up his sleeve," he told the Producer commandingly. He removed the hypodermic spraygun from his bag and carefully filled it with a dozen cc's of the anti-dope. He dabbed the man's arm with a shred of cotton, and pressed the spray against his flesh. "Good thing I hung around tonight," the doctor grumbled. "If this man ever got away in this condition—"

"We know, we know," the Producer said testily. "Fix him up and cut the chatter—"

"I saw that show," the doctor said. "Somebody sure fouled up. Probably gave him an overdose."

"We'll get that later," the Producer promised. "Just do your job, Doc."

"I'm through," Stark said crisply. "Put him on that couch over there and raise his legs. He'll come to his senses in about ten minutes—I hope."

Frick and the Producer helped the man to the sofa. He sprawled on it full-length, fingers trailing on the carpet.

"Do you know who he is?" T. D. said, "He's Jerry Spizer."

"Who?"

"Spizer. The big TV star. You remember."

The doctor halted in the process of clasping his bag, and came over to the sofa. He looked at the man's relaxed face. "By God," he said. "You're right. Now what the hell is Spizer doing on a *Thrill Show*?"

The Producer shrugged. "I don't know. I haven't heard anything about him for the past eight or ten years."

"He must have had it tough," Frick said musingly. "I mean, a big star like that on a program like this—"

"What do you mean, 'a program like this'?" The Producer looked displeased. "If the Staff had a nickel's worth of imagination, they would have played this up big—"

"Gosh," said Frick. "That's true. We could have used a credit card—"

"I'll bet he wouldn't have permitted it," the doctor said. "You know what Spizer thought of the *Thrill Show*."

"Yeah?" The Producer's face reddened. "Well, we proved how wrong he was, didn't we? The public was just sick and tired of that namby-pamby stuff. There *had* to be a *Thrill Show*!"

"Sponsors demanded it," Frick said loyally.

"And besides," T. D. added, "if he doesn't like us, what the hell did he sign up for?"

The doctor pursed his lips. "Maybe he was hungry."

Frick said: "He's still not coming around, Doc."

"He'd better," Stark said warningly. "If the anti-dope doesn't work, it could mean a lot of trouble for the *Thrill Show*, Mr. Donnelly—"

The Producer looked frightened. "That's ridiculous. It's got to work. It's *always* worked—"

"You better call your Staff," the doctor said. "Find out what dosage they gave this man. Check his FCC medical authorization. And do it fast, Mr. Donnelly. This is just the kind of thing the FCC can hang you on."

"Thank God I called that meeting!" the Producer said.

"HERE'S the straight poop."

Manford, the *Thrill Show* director, looked briskly around the room. They had gathered around the table in the conference room, the Staff members still hollow-cheeked and shaken by their experience in the Jam.

"This fellow came into the office last week and signed up for a spot in the *Thrill Show*. We needed somebody for the 'Battle of the Sexes' show, and he was a pretty nice-looking guy. A little seedy, maybe. But all right. He gave his right name—here's his record—but nobody on the interviewing staff recognized him. Guess they're all a little too young to remember Jerry Spizer very well—"

"All right," the Producer prodded. "So what happened?"

"Well, just the routine things. The FCC medical officer gave him the standard physical. His psych check wasn't the best we've ever had, but that's always a debatable business. When he showed up for work yesterday, we gave him the regular dose of ten cc's of adrenaline and four cc's of hypnomecholyl. That's s.o.p. for an Anger-Emotion Show, of course."

The Producer looked at Stark. "Did you give him the shot?"

"No." The doctor shuffled the papers in his hands. "That new fellow, Grayson. Do you want to see him?"

"He's gone home," Manford said. "It'll take an hour to get him here. Why not phonescreen him?"

They took the Director's suggestion. In a few minutes, the image of Dr. Phil Grayson appeared on Phonescreen Four. He was a young man, with a high, balding forehead and a rabbity mustache. He looked worried when his home screen brought him the picture of the intense group around the conference table.

"What is it?" he said.

"Just checking back on some records, Doctor," T. D. said smoothly. "Remember the man you injected today? This fellow Spizer, for the 'Battle of the Sexes' Show?"

The doctor nodded. "Of course."

"Was there anything unusual about the dosage?"

Grayson looked puzzled. "Naturally not. I gave him the prescribed dosage, just like Dr. Stark told me. Ten cc's of nor-adrenaline, forty-four cc's of that—what d'you call it—hypnomecholyl. Why?"

Dr. Stark paled. "I told you that?" he said. The color rushed back into his cheeks a bright crimson. "I told you *adrenaline,* you fool... Not nor-adrenaline! And *four* cc's of hypnomecholyl." He looked wildly at the men around the table. "I swear I told him!" he said.

"You didn't!" the young doctor gasped. "You told me forty-four—"

Stark jumped to his feet, his face livid. He started towards the phonescreen as if to throttle the two-dimensional image on the glass.

"You're a liar!" he cried. "You knew it was an Anger-Emotion Show! You knew what was required—"

"I *didn't* know," Grayson answered, his mustache twitching. "You didn't tell me that. I just assumed—"

"You assumed!" The Producer stood up, looking thunderclouds at Dr. Stark. "You knew what kind of show it was, Stark. Why didn't you tell him? We needed an Anger reaction—not Fear! That's what loused up the whole show!"

Manford groaned. "What does *that* matter now? Forty-four cc's of hypnomecholyl! What kind of a doctor *are* you, Grayson? Don't you know you could *kill* a man that way?"

"I—I didn't know. I never worked with these mecholyl drugs. I studied antibiotics—"

"Better if it had killed him," the Producer said darkly. "We might have covered *that* up. But we can never get him past the FCC examining officer now—"

"I swear he told me forty-four! I swear it!"

Dr. Stark made a rush at the phonescreen. Grayson backed away in terror, despite the many miles that were between him and Stark's intended violence. With a snarl, the older doctor reached up and turned off the instrument.

"Now we're in for it," he told the others.

"Maybe he'll be all right," Manford said. "Maybe he'll snap out of it. A little more anti-dope—"

"Nonsense," Stark snapped. "If it hasn't worked by now, it'll never work. The overdose has permanently affected his nervous system. He's an amnesiac for good—an amnesiac with a permanent case of the jitters—"

Frick shivered. "God! What a fate!"

The Producer looked wise. "Yes," he said solemnly. "He'd be better off dead, wouldn't he?"

The Staff stared at him.

"You know what I'm talking about," T. D. said. "He'd be better off dead. Better for him, for the *Thrill Show*, for us."

"Well," Manford said feebly.

"Well, nothing!" The Producer's voice was harsh. "Do you get the significance of all this? Do you know what happens when the FCC medical officer wants to re-check Spizer? An injunction! A court battle! Then Spizer goes on the stand as Exhibit A, and we lose. No more *Thrill Show.*" He looked at their faces individually. "No more jobs. Bankruptcy. Poverty. The Jam."

This time, the shiver was collective.

"We can't let that happen!" Manford licked his lips. "What about the sponsors? They got pull, don't they? They need us, don't they? I mean, nothing else will give 'em the kind of ratings they get from the *Thrill Show*—"

"Their hands will be tied," T. D. said. "One slip is all the Federal boys have been waiting for. And with all that foreign criticism our State Department's been getting—"

"They still buy our films abroad," another Staff man said glumly.

"That won't matter." The Producer sat down heavily, and put the cold end of his hookahmatic in his mouth. "The *Thrill Show* is doomed. Let's face it."

The group dropped their eyes to the table.

"Of course," the Producer said quietly. "There's one way out.

They looked up at him hopefully.

"Remember Juan Esprenzo?" he said.

They stared at him.

"That was a troublesome situation, too. But we came out of that one, didn't we?"

They gaped, silently.

"Juan Esprenzo was killed on the 'Angry City' *Thrill Show* of November 19th, 1985. It was purely an accident, of course. He wandered out of the guidepaths in the studio and was struck by a falling prop. Nobody could have foreseen it, and nobody could have prevented it. His family received $50,000 in insurance. The FCC investigation described the incident as unfortunate, and there was a special Juan Esprenzo Memorial Show held on January 3rd. But these things happen—just as they once did in boxing, football, racing. Nothing unusual. Nothing to ban a program about."

They turned their eyes to the outer room, where Jerry Spizer lay in a coma on the studio sofa.

"Do you get what I mean?" the Producer said. "Don't you think we could pass another investigation *a la* Esprenzo—better than we could pass the one we're facing right now?"

They looked hopeful and frightened in turn.

"You mean—deliberately *kill* him, T. D.?"

"*Cause* an accident?"

"Kill him right on the program?"

"Exactly," the Producer said, with a satisfied smile. "Put him on again tomorrow night. Make it a set-up. Have something go wrong. Then keep the cameras trained on him while we rush out of the Studio Control Room to find out if he's all right. The whole country will see it was an accident—only an accident."

He turned to Wilson, the head scriptwriter.

"Wilson," he said. "You've got an assignment."

HE AWOKE in darkness, trembling with the thought of escape.

His hands groped around the floor, trying its solidity. When his fingertips found a wall, he raised himself with agonizing slowness, his nails scraping along the ridges in the damp stone.

He pressed his hot cheek against the cool surface, and sobbed pitifully.

When his eyes adjusted to the feeble light, he measured the strength of his prison, and felt the added terror of hopelessness. He turned his eyes to the pool of darkness in the center of the dungeon, and ventured forth a cautious foot.

He had taken only three steps before he heard the voice.

"Look out!" it said. Then he saw the Pit.

He looked with the horror at the writhing beasts inside.

He sank to his knees, and stared in terrible fascination at their swaying bodies. Then he buried his face in his hands.

He looked up when he heard the *swish!* above him.

Gleaming, swinging, evoking a memory in an impossibly distant past—it was a pendulum of razor-sharp steel.

And it was descending.

He screamed, and lifted his arms above his head. The pendulum ground to a halt, the mechanism groaning and screeching in protest. There was a second of silence, and then the blade fell to earth with the suddenness of an avenging sword. This time, the scream was cut off in his throat, and the giant weapon flattened him sickeningly against the edge of the precipice.

Vaguely, as in a dream, he heard the sound of speech, and running footsteps.

"My God! It broke! The pendulum broke!"

"Somebody get the doctor!"

"Look out for that Pit! It's a forty-foot drop!"

"Come on!"

A hand touched his shoulder, and a ring of anxious faces floated like pink balloons over his head.

"I think he's still alive!"

"What?"

"He can't be! That thing weighs a ton!"

"Well, he looks pretty bad, but I can see his eyes moving and he seems to be—"

"Get that blade off him!" He knew that the great weight had been removed from his body, but he could feel no difference. He was looking with almost objective interest into the face of a fat man, a familiar face with wide eyes and an open, bow-lipped mouth. The face was covered with a film of nervous perspiration, and there was a strange sort of anxiety in the man's movements.

"He's got to be! He's got to be!" The fat man was whispering intently.

"But T. D.—"

"Shut up! When you lift him up, I want you to—"

He heard nothing more, but his eyes remained open, fixing the face of the fat man. Then he felt arms around his shoulders once more, and he felt himself slipping, slipping back towards the edge.

With a spurt of strength, with a flash of sudden intelligence, he raised his left arm, and the fingers caught the collar surrounding fat man's neck in loose folds. He held on grimly, until the fat man screamed with satisfying terror.

"Look out, T. D.!" somebody shrieked.

"He's dragging me with him!" The fat man flailed out helplessly. "He's pulling me over the edge!"

Somebody else leaped to his aid, but the dying man's grip was tenacious, his purpose certain.

"*We're going over!*"

They did: the fat man and his victim, and Cameras Three, Four, and Five caught the action beautifully.

MISS STITCH slipped her compact back into her purse, and straightened the corners of the stack of mail on her desk blotter. She looked towards the empty office of the Producer, and smiled with secretive pleasure. Then she slit open the envelopes in front of her, and leisurely read the morning mail.

"Dear Mr. Donnelly... Boy, oh boy! What a thriller you gave us the other night! I thought 'Pit and the Pendulum' was one of the best *Thrill Shows* yet... I sure was disappointed when I saw the title card and thought you were going to re-hash that old Poe bit, but that new ending of yours really knocked me cold... I sure got a kick out of seeing that fat old guy going over the edge of the Pit. What a terrific wind-up! ...I wonder if you would be interested in a really great story idea?... You see, there's this crazy old guy who has a secret laboratory on a mountaintop... Well, one night it's raining and lightning like mad... And this beautiful blonde comes along in a classy convertible..."

THE END

The Men Return

By
JACK VANCE

*Alpha caught a handful of air, a globe of blue liquid, a rock,
kneaded them together...*

THE RELICT came furtively down the crag, a shambling
gaunt creature with tortured eyes. He moved in a series of
quick dashes, using panels of dark air for concealment, running behind each passing shadow, at times crawling on all
fours, head low to the ground. Arriving at the final low out-
crop of rock, he halted and peered across the plain.

Far away rose low hills, blurring into the sky, which was
mottled and sallow like poor milk-glass. The intervening
plain spread like rotten velvet, black-green and wrinkled,
streaked with ocher and rust. A fountain of liquid rock jetted
high in the air, branched out into black coral. In the middle
distance a family of gray objects evolved with a sense of
purposeful destiny: spheres melted into pyramids, became
domes, tufts of white spires, sky-piercing poles; then, as a
final *tour de force*, tesseracts.

The Relict cared nothing for this; he needed food and out
on the plain were plants. They would suffice in lieu of
anything better. They grew in the ground, or sometimes on a
floating lump of water, or surrounding a core of hard black
gas. There were dank black flaps of leaf, clumps of haggard
thorn, pale green bulbs, stalks with leaves and contorted
flowers. There were no recognizable species, and the Relict
had no means of knowing if the leaves and tendrils he had
eaten yesterday would poison him today.

He tested the surface of the plain with his foot. The glassy surface (though it likewise seemed a construction of red and gray-green pyramids) accepted his weight, then suddenly sucked at his leg. In a frenzy he tore himself free, jumped back, squatted on the temporarily solid rock.

Hunger rasped at his stomach. He must eat. He contemplated the plain. Not too far away a pair of Organisms played—sliding, diving, dancing, striking flamboyant poses. Should they approach he would try to kill one of them. They resembled men, and so should make a good meal.

He waited. A long time? A short time? It might have been either; duration had neither quantitative nor qualitative reality. The sun had vanished, and there was no standard cycle or recurrence. Time was a word blank of meaning.

MATTERS had not always been so. The Relict retained a few tattered recollections of the old days, before system and logic had been rendered obsolete. Man had dominated Earth by virtue of a single assumption: that an effect could be traced to a cause, itself the effect of a previous cause.

Manipulation of this basic law yielded rich results; there seemed no need for any other tool or instrumentality. Man congratulated himself on his generalized structure. He could live on desert, on plain or ice, in forest or in city; Nature had not shaped him to a special environment.

He was unaware of his vulnerability. Logic was the special environment; the brain was the special tool.

Then came the terrible hour when Earth swam into a pocket of non-causality, and all the ordered tensions of cause-effect dissolved. The special tool was useless; it had no purchase on reality. From the two billions of men, only a few survived—the mad. They were now the Organisms, lords of the era, their discords so exactly equivalent to the vagaries of the land as to constitute a peculiar wild wisdom. Or perhaps the disorganized matter of the world, loose from the old organization, was peculiarly sensitive to psycho-kinesis.

A handful of others, the Relicts, managed to exist, but only through a delicate set of circumstances. They were the ones most strongly charged with the old causal dynamic. It persisted sufficiently to control the metabolism of their bodies, but could extend no further. They were fast dying out, for sanity provided no leverage against the environment. Sometimes their own minds sputtered and jangled, and they would go raving and leaping out across the plain.

The Organisms observed with neither surprise nor curiosity; how could surprise exist? The mad Relict might pause by an Organism, and try to duplicate the creature's existence. The Organism ate a mouthful of plant; so did the Relict. The Organism rubbed his feet with crushed water; so did the Relict. Presently the Relict would die of poison or rent bowels or skin lesions, while the Organism relaxed in the dank black grass. Or the Organism might seek to eat the Relict; and the Relict would run off in terror, unable to abide any part of the world—running, bounding, breasting the thick air; eyes wide, mouth open, calling and gasping until finally he foundered in a pool of black iron or blundered into a vacuum pocket, to bat around like a fly in a bottle.

The Relicts now numbered very few. Finn, he who crouched on the rock overlooking the plain, lived with four others. Two of these were old men and soon would die. Finn likewise would die unless he found food.

OUT ON THE PLAIN one of the Organisms, Alpha, sat down, caught a handful of air, a globe of blue liquid, a rock, kneaded them together, pulled the mixture like taffy, gave it a great heave. It uncoiled from his hand like rope. The Relict crouched low. No telling what deviltry would occur to the creature. He and all the rest of them—unpredictable! The

Relict valued their flesh as food; but they also would eat him if opportunity offered. In the competition he was at a great disadvantage. Their random acts baffled him. If, seeking to escape, he ran, the worst terror would begin. The direction he set his face was seldom the direction the varying frictions of the ground let him move. But the Organisms were as random and uncommitted as the environment, and the double set of vagaries sometimes compounded, sometimes canceled each other. In the latter case the Organisms might catch him...

It was inexplicable. But then, what was not? The word "explanation" had no meaning.

They were moving toward him; had they seen him? He flattened himself against the sullen yellow rock.

The two Organisms paused not far away. He could hear their sounds, and crouched, sick from conflicting pangs of hunger and fear.

Alpha sank to his knees, lay flat on his back, arms and legs flung out at random, addressing the sky in a series of musical cries, sibilants, guttural groans. It was a personal language he had only now improvised, but Beta understood him well.

"A vision," cried Alpha. "I see past the sky. I see knots, spinning circles. They tighten into hard points; they will never come undone."

Beta perched on a pyramid, glanced over his shoulder at the mottled sky.

"An intuition," chanted Alpha, "a picture out of the other time. It is hard, merciless, inflexible."

Beta poised on the pyramid, dove through the glassy surface, swam under Alpha, emerged, lay flat beside him.

"Observe the Relict on the hillside. In his blood is the whole of the old race—the narrow men with minds like cracks. He has exuded the intuition. Clumsy thing—a blunderer," said Alpha.

"They are all dead, all of them," said Beta. "Although three or four remain." (When *past, present* and *future* are no more than ideas left over from another era, like boots on a dry lake—then the completion of a process can never be defined.)

Alpha said, "This is the vision. I see the Relicts swarming the Earth; then whisking off to nowhere, like gnats in the wind. This is behind us."

The Organisms lay quiet, considering the vision.

A rock, or perhaps a meteor, fell from the sky, struck into the surface of the pond. It left a circular hole, which slowly closed. From another part of the pool a gout of fluid splashed into the air, floated away.

Alpha spoke: "Again—the intuition comes strong! There will be lights in the sky."

The fever died in him. He hooked a finger into the air, hoisted himself to his feet.

Beta lay quiet. Slugs, ants, flies, beetles were crawling on him, boring, breeding. Alpha knew that Beta could arise, shake off the insects, stride off. But Beta seemed to prefer passivity. That was well enough. He could produce another Beta should he choose, or a dozen of him. Sometimes the world swarmed with Organisms, all sorts, all colors, tall as steeples, short and squat as flowerpots.

"I feel a lack," said Alpha. "I will eat the Relict." He set forth, and sheer chance brought him near to the ledge of yellow rock. Finn the Relict sprang to his feet in panic.

ALPHA tried to communicate, so that Finn might pause while Alpha ate. But Finn had no grasp for the many-valued overtones of Alpha's voice. He seized a rock, hurled it at Alpha. The rock puffed into a cloud of dust, blew back into the Relict's face.

Alpha moved closer, extended his long arms. The Relict

kicked. His feet went out from under him, and he slid out on the plain. Alpha ambled complacently behind him. Finn began to crawl away. Alpha moved off to the right—one direction was as good as another. He collided with Beta, and began to eat Beta instead of the Relict. The Relict hesitated; then approached and, joining Alpha, pushed chunks of pink flesh into his mouth.

Alpha said to the Relict, "I was about to communicate an intuition to him whom we dine upon. I will speak to you."

Finn could not understand Alpha's personal language. He ate as rapidly as possible.

Alpha spoke on. "There will be lights in the sky. The great lights."

Finn rose to his feet and, warily watching Alpha, seized Beta's legs, began to pull him toward the hill. Alpha watched with quizzical unconcern.

It was hard work for the spindly Relict. Sometimes Beta floated; sometimes he wafted off on the air; sometimes he adhered to the terrain. At last he sank into a knob of granite which froze around him. Finn tried to jerk Beta loose, and then to pry him up with a stick, without success.

He ran back and forth in an agony of indecision. Beta began to collapse, wither, like a jellyfish on hot sand. The Relict abandoned the hulk. Too late, too late! Food going to waste! The world was a hideous place of frustration!

TEMPORARILY his belly was full. He started back up the crag, and presently found the camp, where the four other Relicts waited—two ancient males, two females. The females, Gisa and Reak, like Finn, had been out foraging. Gisa had brought in a slab of lichen; Reak a bit of nameless carrion.

The old men, Boad and Tagart, sat quietly waiting either for food or for death.

The women greeted Finn sullenly. "Where is the food you went forth to find?"

"I had a whole carcass," said Finn. "I could not carry it."

Boad had slyly stolen the slab of lichen and was cramming it into his mouth. It came alive, quivered and exuded a red ichor which was poison, and the old man died.

"Now there is food," said Finn. "Let us eat."

But the poison created a putrescence; the body seethed with blue foam, flowed away of its own energy.

The women turned to look at the other old man, who said in a quavering voice, "Eat me if you must—but why not choose Reak, who is younger than I?"

Reak, the younger of the women, gnawing on the bit of carrion, made no reply.

Finn said hollowly, "Why do we worry ourselves? Food is ever more difficult, and we are the last of all men."

"No, no," spoke Reak. "Not the last. We saw others on the green mound."

"That was long ago," said Gisa. "Now they are surely dead."

"Perhaps they have found a source of food," suggested Reak.

Finn rose to his feet, looked across the plain. "Who knows? Perhaps there is a more pleasant land beyond the horizon."

"There is nothing anywhere but waste and evil creatures," snapped Gisa.

"What could be worse than here?" Finn argued calmly.

No one could find grounds for disagreement.

"Here is what I propose," said Finn. "Notice this tall peak. Notice the layers of hard air. They bump into the peak, they bounce off, they float in and out and disappear past the edge of sight. Let us all climb this peak, and when a sufficiently large bank of air passes, we will throw ourselves on top, and allow it to carry us to the beautiful regions which may exist just out of sight."

There was argument. The old man Tagart protested his feebleness; the women derided the possibility of the bountiful regions Finn envisioned, but presently, grumbling and arguing, they began to clamber up the pinnacle.

IT TOOK a long time; the obsidian was soft as jelly, and Tagart several times professed himself at the limit of his endurance. But still they climbed, and at last reached the pinnacle. There was barely room to stand. They could see in all directions, far out over the landscape, till vision was lost in the watery gray.

The women bickered and pointed in various directions, but there was small sign of happier territory. In one direction blue-green hills shivered like bladders full of oil. In another direction lay a streak of black—a gorge or a lake of clay. In another direction were blue-green hills—the same they had seen in the first direction; somehow there had been a shift. Below was the plain, gleaming like an iridescent beetle, here and there pocked with black velvet spots, overgrown with questionable vegetation.

They saw Organisms, a dozen shapes loitering by ponds, munching vegetable pods or small rocks or insects. There came Alpha. He moved slowly, still awed by his vision, ignoring the other Organisms. Their play went on, but presently they stood quiet, sharing the oppression.

On the obsidian peak, Finn caught hold of a passing filament of air, drew it in. "Now—all on, and we sail away to the Land of Plenty."

"No," protested Gisa, "there is no room, and who knows if it will fly in the right direction?"

"Where is the right direction?" asked Finn. "Does anyone know?"

No one knew, but the women still refused to climb aboard the filament. Finn turned to Tagart. "Here, old one, show these women how it is; climb on!"

"No, no," he cried. "I fear the air; this is not for me."

"Climb on, old man, then we follow."

Wheezing and fearful, clenching his hands deep into the spongy mass, Tagart pulled himself out onto the air, spindly shanks hanging over into nothing. "Now," spoke Finn, "who next?"

The women still refused. "You go then, yourself," cried Gisa.

"And leave you, my last guarantee against hunger? Aboard now!"

"No— The air is too small; let the old one go and we will follow on a larger."

"Very well." Finn released his grip. The air floated off over the plain, Tagart straddling and clutching for dear life.

They watched him curiously. "Observe," said Finn, "how fast and easily moves the air. Above the Organisms, over all the slime and uncertainty."

But the air itself was uncertain, and the old man's raft dissolved. Clutching at the departing wisps, Tagart sought to hold his cushion together. It fled from under him, and he fell.

ON THE PEAK the three watched the spindly shape flap and twist on its way to earth far below.

"Now," Reak exclaimed vexatiously, "we even have no more meat."

"None," said Gisa, "except the visionary Finn himself."

They surveyed Finn. Together they would more than outmatch him.

"Careful," cried Finn. "I am the last of the Men. You are my women, subject to my orders."

196

They ignored him, muttering to each other, looking at him from the side of their faces. "Careful!" cried Finn. "I will throw you both from this peak."

"That is what we plan for you," said Gisa.

They advanced with sinister caution.

"Stop! I am the last Man!"

"We are better off without you."

"One moment! Look at the Organisms!"

The women looked. The Organisms stood in a knot, staring at the sky.

"Look at the sky!"

The women looked; the frosted glass was cracking, breaking, curling aside.

"The blue! The blue sky of old times!"

A terribly bright light burnt down, seared their eyes. The rays warmed their naked backs.

"The sun," they said in awed voices. "The sun has come back to Earth."

The shrouded sky was gone; the sun rode proud and bright in a sea of blue. The ground below churned, cracked, heaved, solidified. They felt the obsidian harden under their feet; its color shifted to glossy black. The Earth, the sun, the galaxy, had departed the region of freedom; the other time with its restrictions and logic was once more with them.

"This is Old Earth," cried Finn. "We are Men of Old Earth! The land is once again ours!"

"And what of the Organisms?"

"If this is the Earth of old, then let the Organisms beware!"

The Organisms stood on a low rise of ground beside a runnel of water that was rapidly becoming a river flowing out onto the plain.

Alpha cried, "Here is my intuition! It is exactly as I knew. The freedom is gone; the tightness, the constriction are back!"

"How will we defeat it?" asked another Organism.

"Easily," said a third. "Each must fight a part of the battle. I plan to hurl myself at the sun, and blot it from existence." And he crouched, threw himself into the air. He fell on his back and broke his neck.

"The fault," said Alpha, "is in the air; because the air surrounds all things."

Six Organisms ran off in search of air and, stumbling into the river, drowned.

"In any event," said Alpha, "I am hungry." He looked around for suitable food. He seized an insect, which stung him. He dropped it. "My hunger remains."

He spied Finn and the two women descending from the crag. "I will eat one of the Relicts," he said. "Come, let us all eat."

Three of them started off as usual in random directions. By chance Alpha came face to face with Finn. He prepared to eat, but Finn picked up a rock. The rock remained a rock, hard, sharp, heavy. Finn swung it down, taking joy in the inertia. Alpha died with a crushed skull. One of the other Organisms attempted to step across a crevasse twenty feet wide and disappeared into it; the other sat down, swallowed rocks to assuage his hunger, and presently went into convulsions.

Finn pointed here and there around the fresh new land. "In that quarter, the new city, like that of the Legends. Over here the farms, the cattle."

"We have none of these," protested Gisa.

"No," said Finn. "Not now. But once more the sun rises and sets, once more rock has weight and air has none. Once more water falls as rain and flows to the sea." He stepped forward over the fallen Organism. "Let us make plans."

THE END

If you've enjoyed this book, you will not want to miss these terrific titles...

ARMCHAIR SCI-FI, FANTASY, & HORROR DOUBLE NOVELS, $12.95 each

D-1 **THE GALAXY RAIDERS** by William P. McGivern
SPACE STATION #1 by Frank Belknap Long

D-2 **THE PROGRAMMED PEOPLE** by Jack Sharkey
SLAVES OF THE CRYSTAL BRAIN by William Carter Sawtelle

D-3 **YOU'RE ALL ALONE** by Fritz Leiber
THE LIQUID MAN by Bernard C. Gilford

D-4 **CITADEL OF THE STAR LORDS** by Edmund Hamilton
VOYAGE TO ETERNITY by Milton Lesser

D-5 **IRON MEN OF VENUS** by Don Wilcox
THE MAN WITH ABSOLUTE MOTION by Noel Loomis

D-6 **WHO SOWS THE WIND...** by Rog Phillips
THE PUZZLE PLANET by Robert A. W. Lowndes

D-7 **PLANET OF DREAD** by Murray Leinster
TWICE UPON A TIME by Charles L. Fontenay

D-8 **THE TERROR OUT OF SPACE** by Dwight V. Swain
QUEST OF THE GOLDEN APE by Ivar Jorgensen and Adam Chase

D-9 **SECRET OF MARRACOTT DEEP** by Henry Slesar
PAWN OF THE BLACK FLEET by Mark Clifton.

D-10 **BEYOND THE RINGS OF SATURN** by Robert Moore Williams
A MAN OBSESSED by Alan E. Nourse

ARMCHAIR SCIENCE FICTION CLASSICS, $12.95 each

C-1 **THE GREEN MAN**
by Harold M. Sherman

C-2 **A TRACE OF MEMORY**
By Keith Laumer

ARMCHAIR MASTERS OF SCIENCE FICTION SERIES, $16.95 each

M-1 **MASTERS OF SCIENCE FICTION, Vol. One**
Bryce Walton—"Dark of the Moon" and other tales

M-2 **MASTERS OF SCIENCE FICTION, Vol. Two**
Jerome Bixby: "One Way Street" and other tales

If you've enjoyed this book, you will not want to miss these terrific titles...

ARMCHAIR SCI-FI & HORROR DOUBLE NOVELS, $12.95 each

D-11   **PERIL OF THE STARMEN** by Kris Neville
THE STRANGE INVASION by Murray Leinster

D-12   **THE STAR LORD** by Boyd Ellanby
CAPTIVES OF THE FLAME by Samuel R. Delaney

D-13   **MEN OF THE MORNING STAR** by Edmund Hamilton
PLANET FOR PLUNDER by Hal Clement and Sam Merwin, Jr.

D-14   **ICE CITY OF THE GORGON** by Chester S. Geier and Richard S. Shaver
WHEN THE WORLD TOTTERED by Lester Del Rey

D-15   **WORLDS WITHOUT END** by Clifford D. Simak
THE LAVENDER VINE OF DEATH by Don Wilcox

D-16   **SHADOW ON THE MOON** by Joe Gibson
ARMAGEDDON EARTH by Geoff St. Reynard

D-17   **THE GIRL WHO LOVED DEATH** by Paul W. Fairman
SLAVE PLANET by Laurence M. Janifer

D-18   **SECOND CHANCE** by J. F. Bone
MISSION TO A DISTANT STAR by Frank Belknap Long

D-19   **THE SYNDIC** by C. M. Kornbluth
FLIGHT TO FOREVER by Poul Anderson

D-20   **SOMEWHERE I'LL FIND YOU** by Milton Lesser
THE TIME ARMADA by Fox B. Holden

ARMCHAIR SCIENCE FICTION CLASSICS, $12.95 each

C-3   **INTO PLUTONIAN DEPTHS**
by Stanton A. Coblentz

C-4   **CORPUS EARTHLING**
by Louis Charbonneau

C-5   **THE TIME DISSOLVER**
by Jerry Sohl

C-6   **WEST OF THE SUN**
by Edgar Pangborn

ARMCHAIR SCIENCE FICTION & HORROR GEMS SERIES, $12.95 each

G-1   **SCIENCE FICTION GEMS, Vol. One**
Isaac Asimov and others

G-2   **HORROR GEMS, Vol. One**
Carl Jacobi and others